# TOGETHER AT RUBY'S

KC LUCK

This book is a work of fiction. Names, characters, places, and incidents are products of the author's imagination and/or are used fictitiously. Any resemblance to actual events, locales or persons either living or dead is entirely coincidental.

Copyright © 2023 KC Luck Media

All rights reserved, including the right to reproduce this book or portions thereof in any form whatsoever

# 1

*E*njoying the warm June sun on her face, Liza Martinez walked through the busy, open-air corridors of the outlet mall a half hour south of her home in Portland, Oregon. Navigating the throngs of people all eager to find a good deal, she was flanked by Allie and Rey, her two best friends. All three had a spring in their step after some very successful shopping. All the summer fashions were already on discount, and Liza was particularly pleased with her finds, especially a pair of strappy, white and tan sandals that would go perfectly with the light green sundress she planned to wear that evening. Being a Sunday, it was date night with the love of her life, Tate Nilsen, and she knew the woman was especially fond of the color, particularly on Liza.

The trio headed for the parking lot, laden with multiple shopping bags from a variety of stores, yet Liza saw one more place she needed to stop by for a minute or two. "I know we said we would be out of here by four p.m., but can we please take a look at the jewelry shop?" Liza asked. "Only for a second, I promise."

Allie laughed. "Now why are you interested in going there?" she teased, and Liza smiled at her friend's question.

"You know exactly why, Allie Dawson," she answered, but before she said anything more, Rey playfully bumped her shoulder.

"It wouldn't be to look at engagement rings, now would it?" Rey asked. "For the hundredth time."

Liza gave her friend's comment some consideration. *I think I may have looked more than a hundred times,* she thought. *I'm an expert on diamonds now.* She stopped walking, and when the other two did the same, Liza looked from one friend to the other. "Tate is going to propose to me any minute, I just know it," she said. "But I have no idea what kind of ring she bought, so I need to look at some examples. I think you should both be rather interested too. It's not like you two don't have special people in your lives."

Rey's eyes widened. "I think that's a little more than I would expect," she said, but Liza saw a hint of a blush on her cheeks. She was so happy Rey and Marty were finally a serious couple and not only roommates. They seemed to take forever to figure out their true feelings, but then the two were not like Liza. She never hesitated to say how she felt about anything. When she met Tate, Liza knew immediately that she was the one. Years ago, Allie had invited her to what had been the Ruby Slipper after the college class they shared. One look at the quiet and handsome, dark-haired woman sitting in the horseshoe booth along with all Allie's closest friends took Liza's breath away. She had been quick to let Tate know it, and luckily, the feeling was mutual.

Starting to walk toward the jewelry store, Allie shook her head. "I don't expect anything either," she said. "But it's always fun to look."

"Thank you," Liza said, always loving getting her way,

even when it was only with her best friends. "We will be in and out quickly. Ten minutes tops."

Rey held the door open for Liza and Allie. "We'll see," she said, but there was a twinkle in her eye. "I just love seeing you so happy."


WIPING away the sheen of sweat on her face with a white gym towel, Tate worked to catch her breath. Her heart had a rapid beat, but she felt it slowing already. After setting a personal 5k running record on the treadmill, she felt good, really good. She took pride in being physically fit, more muscular than average, but also never wanted anyone to think she showed off. Her friend, Nikki, teased her at times about the attention she attracted when she bench pressed a considerable weight, but the act was never intended to draw a crowd. According to her friend, more than one woman in the gym had their eyes on Tate. That meant nothing to her. She was only interested in one person, the woman who made up her world, and that was Liza Martinez.

"New personal record today?" Nikki asked as Tate joined her at the weight bench.

Tate nodded. "Yes," she said. "By eleven seconds."

Holding up her hand for a high five, Nikki grinned. "Outstanding," she said as Tate slapped their hands together. She appreciated her friend's excitement over the accomplishment. They worked out early almost every morning at Tate's favorite gym. If she could call anyone her best friend, it would be Nikki Vander. Although the woman was tall, blonde, extremely attractive, and had a body almost as fit as Tate, Nikki was surprisingly humble and had a heart of gold. If Tate ever needed anything, she could turn to her friend any time day or night. In fact, all the friends in Tate's closeknit circle knew Nikki would always be there for them. In some ways, the woman was the glue that held their group together. That and the bar called Ruby's, which aside from her love for her gym, Tate considered a second home.

Nights when she wasn't working late, she would meet Liza at Ruby's and check in with her friends. Unfortunately, over the last two years, those opportunities were few and far between. As much as she wished it didn't, her job consumed her life as she scratched and clawed her way up the ladder at the large, international financial firm where she had worked since she was a college intern a decade ago. *But that's all about to change*, she thought as she picked up one of the large, round metal plates to slide onto the waiting barbell. *Because tomorrow I'll be the new Vice President of Mergers and Acquisitions.* A smile spread across her face simply thinking about how much better life would be after tomorrow morning—hers and Liza's.

"I don't know what you're thinking, my friend," Nikki said from where she stood beside the weight bench ready to spot Tate when she was ready to lift. "But from that smile, I think it's pretty damn good."

Taking her place on the bench, Tate lay back and positioned herself under the heavily laden bar. "You're right," she said. "It is."

"That's all I get?" Nikki asked while Tate got a good grip.

"Yep," she said in her usual stoic style. As much as she wanted to share the news with her friend, Tate didn't want to jinx getting the promotion. She knew most people would find that line of thinking silly, but she grew up in a house where superstitions were taken seriously. Her mom even went so far as to perform a little "white magic" from time to time. Tate remembered candles of various colors lit on specific occasions, finding crystals in odd places around the house, and attending celebrations at the solstices and equinoxes. Only Liza knew the truth about the new position, and Tate had sworn her to secrecy.

As Liza, Allie, and Rey discussed the pros and cons of each sparkling engagement ring in the jewelry store's many glass display cases, Liza hardly contained her excitement. Tate was certain to propose to her once she got her new position at work. More than once, Liza had to bite her tongue to keep from blurting out the news of Tate's upcoming promotion. Only her promise to Tate kept her quiet. The woman had made her cross her heart that she wouldn't say anything before there was a done deal. *Another one of her crazy superstitions*, Liza thought as the trio moved to the last case where less traditional rings were on display. *I will never understand how someone so focused on the world of facts and figures can believe all that stuff.* Still, she loved Tate, even for her sometimes peculiar ideas, and would never break her word to her.

Stopping to look, Liza took in the sight of her favorite. A one and half carat, round-cut diamond rimmed with rubies that seemed to glow under the perfectly placed lighting. The beauty of the ring against the cream-colored velvet always made her stop and appreciate it.

"That's the ring, isn't it?" Allie said in a hushed voice, as if the bit of beautiful jewelry needed to be revered.

Liza nodded. "I think the ring is about perfect," she answered. "Not too big, not too small."

"It is very beautiful," Rey agreed before tilting her head. "But how will Tate know you like this one so much?"

Sighing, Liza stepped away from the display case to lead them to the exit. "Well, I have dropped hints now and then about what I like in rings, but I am never sure what sinks in with Tate," she replied. "She's always so calm about everything."

Allie followed Liza and Rey out the door of the jewelry store. "I always wondered if she was as quiet at home as she was at Ruby's," Allie said.

"Tate is the epitome of the strong, silent type," Liza replied as they started for the mall's vast parking lot. "But it's probably for the best, you know, considering."

Both Rey and Allie laughed as they all scanned the crowded lot for Liza's blue Subaru. "Do you mean considering your… hmm… outgoing personality?" Rey asked, making Liza snort a laugh.

"Well put, Rey," she said, always impressed at how her friend could find the right thing to say in any situation. Thankfully, the woman's tact helped get Liza out of hot water more than once. "But yes, exactly that. No matter how mad I get or what I say, Tate very rarely gets ruffled. It takes a lot for her to lose her temper." If Liza had to describe her partner in a sentence, she would say that Tate was her rock. Regardless of what whirlwind of trouble Liza stirred up, she could always turn to her for unconditional love and support. They were the perfect balance, with only one thing causing trouble between them—how much Tate worked. *But that's about to change,* she thought as they reached the car. *She promised me her schedule would be much more normal after she became the Vice President of Mergers and Acquisitions. No more working sixteen-hour days.* Liza couldn't wait.

2

After wrapping up one of the best workouts Tate had in quite a while, she helped Nikki rack all the weights they used. She felt excellent. The perfect mixture of worked muscles and sense of accomplishment. "Hey, do you have time to grab a smoothie at the counter, or do you have to head out?" Nikki asked once they finished their task. "Because if you have an extra minute, I have a question to ask you."

Tate checked her watch. The time wasn't much past four o'clock, so she had at least a half an hour before heading home to take a hot shower. With Liza shopping, she was pretty confident there was a little time to kill before her girlfriend got home. Besides, if Nikki needed something, she always wanted to help her. Considering how generous Nikki was, it was the least Tate could do.

"Absolutely," Tate said. "Everything okay?"

"Oh yeah," Nikki replied. "I need some of your business wisdom is all."

Curious, while not sure what to make of Nikki's comment about needing advice, Tate followed her to the smoothie counter. "You know I deal with mostly international finance, right?" she asked. "Business school was a long time ago."

After they ordered two protein and fruit smoothies and stepped aside to wait, Nikki nodded. "I know. But it's an investment type question," she said. "I've come into a hefty sum of money and want to put it somewhere useful."

*Hefty sum of money? Like what?* she thought while keeping her face neutral. Always known for her reserved personality, being nosey was way outside of Tate's norm, even with a close friend. "Well," she started. "There are numerous options, of course. It will depend on how much risk you want to take with it mostly."

"I see." Nikki looked thoughtful. "I'll have to think about that."

"Do you want me to run through the options with you?" Tate asked as their order was called. "I can have my assistant set up an appointment."

Finding them a small table, Nikki furrowed her brow. "That might be too formal at this stage," she said and grinned. "I was thinking maybe over beers at Ruby's sometime soon?"

"Even better," Tate answered. "I wish more of my clients were open to that." Taking a drink through the straw, she relished the sweet taste of the thick liquid for a moment before the phone in her pocket buzzed. *Maybe that's Liza home already?* she thought. *Or running late?* She smiled a bit, knowing that was most likely. The text was from Allie, though, and for a second she felt a pang of worry only to read the women were running late.

"A fender bender is holding us up at the 217 exit," Allie wrote. "Liza says she's sorry but will make it up to you."

Tate wasn't surprised since that area of the freeway was notorious for delays. "No problem. Tell her I'll meet her at home," she typed but hesitated with her thumb in the air before adding, "and tell her thank you for not texting while driving."

Allie sent back a smiley face. "Everything okay?" Nikki asked, and Tate nodded as she put away the phone.

"Stuck in traffic," she said, suddenly having an idea since they had extra time to hang out.

The topic was something she had been meaning to ask Nikki for a while, but the whole subject made her nervous. "So, if you have a few more minutes, now I have a question for you."

Swallowing a drink of her smoothie, Nikki winked. "You know me," she said. "I have nothing but time." It was true. Tate did know Nikki was generally available at any time day or night. She had no idea how the woman earned a living or what she did for work, and whenever anyone started to raise the question, Tate noticed Nikki avoided the topic every time. *Just another facet of the mysterious Nikki*, she thought, before building up the courage to ask her question.

She stalled by taking another drink, and Nikki apparently noticed because she raised an eyebrow. "Okay, okay," Tate said, taking a deep breath. "It's about Liza." She cleared her throat but then pushed on. "I want to propose to her, but I have no idea how to do it."


SITTING in the car as traffic crawled along excruciatingly slow, Liza practiced keeping her impatience in check. There was nothing to be done but limp along with everyone else as they all squeezed into one lane to pass the site of the three-car accident. *At least I am here with Allie and Rey to keep me company*, she thought, half listening to their chatter about Portland's upcoming Pride festival and parade. "It lands on your birthday this year though," Rey said, and it took a second for Liza to clue in that the statement was directed toward her. "Will you and Tate be in town for that weekend? Or do you have other plans to do something special?"

"Especially since it's your big-three-oh," Allie added making Liza wince. Her friend was only being playful, but Liza wasn't particularly excited about turning thirty. Her dislike for the significant event wasn't something she elaborated on with her circle, usually choosing to laugh it off as no big deal. But deep down, the upcoming date unsettled her. Clearly, this time Allie noticed her reaction. "Hey, I didn't say that to upset you." Her voice turned gentle. "Are you not looking forward to your birthday? Normally, you love them."

"I know you didn't," Liza said with a sigh. "And no, I'm not looking forward to it this year." Allie was right, Liza did love her birthdays normally. Being the center of attention and showered with gifts made her extremely happy. But leaving her twenties behind was a big deal, and if she was honest, scared her. "I just don't know how I feel about turning thirty. I mean, I expected my life to be a lot different by now."

Always the comforting one, Rey rubbed Liza's leg from beside her in the passenger seat. "In what ways?" she asked. "Married to Tate?"

Nodding, Liza was relieved to finally be moving past the accident on the freeway. "Yes, married for sure," she replied as she accelerated to the normal sixty-five with all three lanes open again. "And, well, if I'm being honest, I hoped to have a kid or two as well." She felt her eyes well with tears. "But I don't have any of that." A tiny tear slipped out.

Leaning forward, Allie touched Liza's shoulder from the backseat. "Liza, I'm so sorry you're feeling sad about it," Allie said. "But all of that is going to change soon. You already said you were sure Tate would propose any day now."

Frustrated at her emotional reaction, Liza swallowed down her sadness and plastered on a smile. "Yes, she will," she said, thinking again of how she wished she could tell her friends about Tate's upcoming promotion. *But I promised*, she thought and let it go. *For now.* "And I absolutely can't wait."

LETTING herself into the three-bedroom house she shared with Liza, Tate was happy to see her girlfriend wasn't home yet. With her gym bag over one shoulder, she carried a bouquet of colorful roses and other summer flowers in her other hand as she crossed the living room. By getting home first, Tate would have time to grab the shower she hoped for as well as be able to leave the surprise arrangement on the kitchen table for Liza to find. No one liked flowers and other tokens of affection more than the woman she lived with. The romantic gesture would be a great way to start their standing date night.

After stashing her bag in the bedroom they had converted into Tate's office, she started to strip while she walked down the hall. By the time she was at the master bathroom, only her briefs and sports bra remained. A shower would feel fantastic on her slightly sore muscles. Not that she minded the feeling of exertion, in fact, she relished it. The sensation meant she had worked hard and that was what Tate did best whether in the gym or at her job. Turning on the water and letting it run warm, she stripped the rest of the way and climbed into the spray. The sting of the hot droplets made her shiver with pleasure. *It's been such a fantastic day,* she thought, reaching for the shampoo. Only a few hours of work this morning, then a long session at her favorite gym, followed by a good talk with Nikki, leading to date night all added up to near perfection.

Thinking back, when Tate asked for help at the gym, she wasn't sure her friend would help her. Nikki had raised her hands as if to ward off Tate's statement and implied question.

"Hold on a second, buddy," Nikki had said. "If you're asking me for advice on how to pull off a wedding proposal, you got the wrong gal." She had grinned her devilish smile. "I love 'em and leave 'em, remember? No marriages for me. Not ever."

"I know," Tate admitted. "But you're also one of the most romantic people I've ever met, so try to stretch your imagination for a few minutes."

Nikki had nodded at the statement. "True," she said. "Okay, I'll help. What exactly are you asking of me?"

With a sigh, Tate drank the last of her smoothie. "Pretty much the where and how."

"Oh, so you know the when?"

Tate thought about the question for a second. She wasn't going to reveal everything about what was happening at work, but a hint couldn't hurt. "Let's just say things are going my way, so I am planning it pretty soon."

After punching Tate playfully on the shoulder, Nikki leaned back in her chair. "That is music to my ears," she said. "Nothing could make me happier than seeing you two get hitched at last."

"Thanks," Tate said with a smile that she felt to her core. "It has taken awhile, which is why I want this to be the greatest proposal ever. Liza's been pretty patient, so she deserves that."

"Hmm," Nikki hummed. "Can I have a few days to think about it? This is a tough one."

Thankful Nikki would help her, Tate had agreed.

# 3

"Tate, I'm home. What an incredible mess traffic was," Liza said when she came rushing into the house from the garage. When there was no answer and Tate was nowhere in sight, she frowned. She was sure her girlfriend was home because her Ford Explorer was parked in their garage. After dropping her many shopping bags on the large sectional couch, she started across the great room for Tate's office a moment before noticing the bouquet of flowers on the dining room table. "Tate! What are these? They are so beautiful." She scooped up the vase and smelled the roses mixed with dahlias and other summer flowers. The yellows, oranges, and pinks looked perfect together. Clearly Tate was home, or at least had been, to leave her the thoughtful surprise.

Before Liza could take the bouquet to the kitchen to add water to the vase, Tate appeared in the doorway leading to the hall and their bedroom. "I'm glad you like them," she said, standing in a navy-blue silk robe with a gold dragon embroidered on the shoulder. She rubbed her damp hair with a fluffy green towel.

"I don't just like them," Liza said, a beaming smile on her face, "I love them. You're so sweet." She went to Tate and gave her a quick kiss on the lips. "Let me put these in water and then I can show you all the stuff I bought today."

Before Liza could turn away, Tate slung her bath towel over her shoulder and lightly caught Liza by the elbow to hold her close. "I think I need more of a thank you kiss than that," she said, in a tone that was both playful and suggestive. Liza paused and took a moment to truly look at her partner. Tousled dark hair that set off her sharp blue eyes. Broad shoulders covered by the thin cloth of her robe. Unable to help but notice the way the fabric outlined Tate's body, Liza had a strong suspicion there wasn't anything on under the silk the woman wore. *She is so sexy,* she thought. *Confident, smart, commanding... everything I love in a partner and what will make her an amazing Vice President of Mergers and Acquisitions.*

Slowly, Liza smiled as a warm tingle ran through her. "Oh really?" she said. "And what sort of kiss would that be?" Without a word, Tate let go of her arm before cupping Liza's face in her hands. She easily but gently pulled Liza's face closer and for a moment, Liza reveled in the woman's strength. Then, Tate kissed her and there was no mistaking the message she was sending. As she took the kiss deeper, using her tongue to tease her, Liza sighed with pleasure. Not only was the kiss fantastic and sexy, but the entire act was a pleasant surprise. Tate was a lot of wonderful things, but rarely spontaneous. First the flowers, and then the kiss left Liza unsure what to think.

Pulling away, Tate let go of Liza's face. "That's better," Tate said with a sultry half smile on her lips. She nodded toward the pile of bags on the couch across the room. "I don't suppose there's any new lingerie in all of those, is there?"

Tossing her head, feeling like she needed to take back

some of the control between them, Liza's eyes narrowed. "There could be," she said, in a suggestive tone of her own. "And what if there is?"

Tate took a step backward toward the bedroom hallway. "Then that's the outfit I want you to model for me first."

As Tate went into the bedroom, she realized it had been a while since she and Liza had made love. *Too long,* she thought, pulling back the lightweight, white quilt on the king-sized bed. *But I'm about to fix that.* Her body tingled with anticipation of being naked, wrapped up with Liza under the sheets. After shrugging off her robe and draping it over a chair, Tate slid under the cool cotton fabric and relished the feel against her bare skin. Immediately her nipples hardened from the contact and the throb between her legs pulsed even harder. Expectations of what lay ahead had her extremely turned on.

Thankfully, Tate didn't have to wait long, and when Liza appeared in the doorway to the bedroom, she had changed her clothes. In the faint, early evening light filtering in through the pulled curtains, Tate saw her new outfit was exactly what she requested—a sexy piece of lingerie. The red and black lace clung to Liza's slender body, stretching tightly across her full breasts. Tate licked her lips as she saw how hard Liza's nipples were under the see-through fabric. Every part of her couldn't wait to put her mouth on one. "Do you like?" Liza asked in a sultry tone.

"I more than like it," Tate replied. "Want to come over here and let me show you how much?"

"Maybe. And if I don't?" Liza asked, although she started to walk toward the bed. "Would you get up and throw me over your shoulder like some sort of Neanderthal?"

A low growl of arousal rose in Tate at the image of easily

picking Liza up and carrying her to bed. "I might," she said and meant it. The vision was erotic and very tempting. *Later, she thought. When she's not expecting it.* For the moment, Liza looked more than willing to come to the bed and join Tate. Before Tate could push the sheet past her hips to invite her lover into the bed, Liza was on top, straddling her. Even through the thin fabric, Tate felt the wet heat between Liza's legs. When the woman ground her body down onto Tate's clit, they both let out a gasp.

The sensation of not quite having skin on skin contact made Tate a little crazy and clearly affected Liza too as she continued to press down. "What do you have in mind?" Liza asked, her voice breathless. "I know you're thinking of something. I can see it in your eyes."

Tate ran her hands up Liza's thighs until she grabbed her hips. "I do have an idea in mind," she said twisting her body enough to open the drawer of the nightstand. Reaching inside she found the long vibrator that she realized they hadn't used in forever. *Unless she uses it on herself when I'm at work late into the evening all the time*, Tate thought. Somehow the vision only made her more excited and changed her thinking a little. A new idea formed, and she turned back to Liza. "I want to use this."

Clearly liking the idea, Liza looked at her through half closed eyes. "Do you?"

With a nod, Tate held it out for her. "But I want to watch you use it on yourself."


TATE HAD NEVER MADE SUCH a request before and Liza wasn't sure how she felt about it. Although she did use the vibrator from time to time when she was missing Tate, she only did so to help herself fall asleep afterward. She never considered using it in front of Tate. Tilting her head, she looked into the woman's eyes. The hunger she saw there helped her decide, but she had conditions too. "If I do," Liza said. "Do you promise to wear your strap-on for me later?"

She was rewarded with a hum of pleasure from Tate's lips. "I promise," she answered. Without another word, Liza took the vibrator from her lover's hand and turned it on low. Keeping her eyes locked with Tate's, she ran the tip of the buzzing shaft over her hard nipple, sucking in a breath at the intense sensation. It was like a bolt of electricity from her breast to her clit.

She gasped. "Like this?"

In answer, Tate lifted her hips to increase the contact between them. "More," she groaned, and with a little laugh of satisfaction at the way she made Tate react, Liza ran the vibrator down her body and over her stomach, until it was poised just above her own throbbing center. Not breaking eye contact with Tate, she lifted herself to her knees so the toy could slide between them. Liza threw her head back with a little cry of delight when the vibration ran across her swollen clit. For a second she thought she might climax from the intensity of the moment, but Tate grabbed her wrist. "Don't come yet. I want more."

Once again, Liza hesitated, never having used the vibrator in quite the position Tate demanded but the idea of something so erotic also made her heart race with excitement. "Okay," she breathed and reached her hand between her legs to pull the snaps free. Nothing was in her way to keep her from going further. Holding her breath, Liza slipped the shaft lower on her body until the toy pushed her lips open wide. She felt how slippery she was. *I am so turned on,* she thought. *Tate has me so wet.* It had been too long since she felt that way and encouraged by her body's reaction, Liza slightly lifted one leg. The position was enough to let Tate have a clear view of what her hand was doing.

Unable to take the sensation of the vibrator's tip against her opening any longer, Liza pushed the toy deeper. Someone moaned but she wasn't sure if it was herself or Tate. No longer timid, Liza slid the shaft as far as it would go inside her. She felt her body tighten around it and knew her orgasm was seconds away. "More," she heard Tate growl and didn't hesitate to start slowly moving the vibrator in and out of her hungry body. The image of what Tate would do to her later only made the sensation more intense. She loved feeling full, feeling taken.

Starting to quiver, Liza moved her hand faster. "Oh Tate, oh baby, I don't think I can wait any longer," she said, almost begging. "Please let me come."

"Not yet," Tate growled. "Go faster. I want you to explode all over me."

Doing as she was told, Liza pumped faster, pressing deeper. "Please, Tate," she begged. "I am going crazy."

"Yes," Tate hissed. "Do it."

As if on cue, a ripple of intensity rolled up Liza's body. She felt her body throbbing around the vibrator as she let herself go with the wave until the orgasm made her scream.

4

If Tate thought she felt good the day before, it was nothing compared to how she felt that morning as she made her way to work. The short commute had gone quicker than normal, and she was so relaxed and happy she hummed along with the radio. Normally, Monday mornings were stressful but not today. *And that has a lot to do with last night*, Tate thought with a grin as she parked. The lovemaking between her and Liza had been off the charts fantastic. *Maybe tonight will be worthy of a repeat.* It was likely the biggest day of her career, possibly her life so far. VP of Mergers and Acquisitions was something she had aspired to since day one at the company. She had worked her ass off to the point she risked her relationship with Liza, but finally the dream was coming true.

Pushing through the revolving door into the lobby of the high-rise and walking by the security desk toward the elevator, she gave a nod to the uniformed guard who sat behind the desk. "You have a spring in your step this morning, Miss Nilsen," he said with a grin.

"Most definitely," she replied as the elevator doors slid

open and she made a dash to join a pack of others. All were dressed in the usual business attire of jackets, slacks, or pencil skirts. Inside were some of her close colleagues, and they all gave her a smile. It was not going to be a surprise when she was announced, and no one was jealous because Tate was not only a team player, but someone to be respected. She was well-liked and trustworthy, not always attributes found in up-and-coming business executives.

The man beside her smiled. "Have a good day," he said, and as she exited the elevator she turned, giving him a wink as the elevator doors closed. Walking to her office, she saw the executive assistant who was assigned to her and a few colleagues. The woman was absolutely beaming. *Everyone seems happy for me today*, she thought, and it made her feel warm inside.

"I have a coffee for you," the assistant said.

Tate stopped at her desk. "You're the best," she said and was about to walk into her glass-walled office when the assistant held up a hand to make her pause.

"Just letting you know, there is an all hands meeting at eight o'clock," she said, and Tate hesitated. *Would they be announcing this to everyone without speaking to me individually first?* she wondered. There had been tons of hints from her boss, but nothing formally offered to her. *Don't get paranoid now. I have nothing to worry about. This is a slam dunk.*

Nodding, Tate let her smile fall back into place. "I will certainly be there."

"As well you should," the assistant said returning the smile. Entering her office, Tate had thirty minutes before the meeting and decided she needed to distract herself. *Maybe I'll start brainstorming Nikki's request for investment advice*, she thought. After leaving the gym yesterday, she had thought about it a little bit but then last night had turned magical and it had flown out of her mind.

Normally, she would advise Nikki to make long-term, conservative financial investments, something like inflation-protected securities, but somehow she knew her friend would find that boring. *And boring is not something Nikki does,* she thought. *Maybe I should have her invest in a business looking to go public in the next six months.* Not necessarily a brand-new startup because that was too risky, but something established and ready to join the big leagues. Something Nikki could invest time in, have input on decisions, and therefore find satisfaction when things went well. Tate's mind turned to Ruby's. She knew Vivian was still working on making the bar a success. The nationally televised New Year's Eve gala months ago had helped, but Tate doubted that solved everything. *But that would be too close to home. I'll have to do some research and find out what is for sale in Portland.* After turning on her computer, she started to search.

Swiping at her eyelashes with the black mascara wand, Liza got ready for work. Mondays were not her favorite, but that morning was better than most. The evening before, and half the night for that matter, had been the best she remembered in a long time. Tate had been unstoppable, and Liza's body tightened as she remembered their love making. *Almost as good as when we first got together,* she thought, checking her reflection in the mirror before putting a little gloss on her lips. *Back when we couldn't seem to get enough of each other.* Smiling at herself, Liza fluffed her styled hair a little, liking how she looked with a healthy glow on her face and a twinkle in her brown eyes. *The only thing that would make this morning better is if I didn't have to go to work at all.*

As she hurried through the house to the kitchen to fill her extra-large travel mug with coffee, the age-old fantasy came to her. She looked forward to a day when she and Tate might be in a place financially where Liza could stop working full time. Instead, she could volunteer at a non-profit or something. *Or be here raising our babies*, she couldn't help but think. That was the real fantasy—to be a stay-at-home mom. Although broaching the subject of someday having kids with Tate always led to frustration, Liza was convinced the heart of the issue was money. Tate wouldn't agree to trying artificial insemination until she was confident she could provide for them.

*But that's all about to be resolved at last,* she thought as she rummaged in her oversized purse looking for her car keys. After the hefty raise that came with the promotion to vice president, there was no way Tate could still believe money was an issue. *Maybe we can go away somewhere tropical soon and talk on a warm, sandy beach about starting a family.* It wasn't like Liza was getting any younger. *Of course, I'd like to get married first, but that's a whole different battle.*

Finally, with coffee and keys in hand, Liza made her way into the house's attached garage. As she approached her Subaru, there was a note under the wiper blade. Plucking it free, she climbed behind the wheel before opening the folded over scrap of yellow notepad paper. "Thank you," was all it said in Tate's crisp, blocky writing. A smile lit up Liza's face. The short message was exactly her lover's style, and the two simple words conveyed a million sentiments.

Picking up her phone, Liza contemplated typing a quick text to Tate. They rarely sent them during the workday because Tate was always so busy and hardly ever answered, but she felt today was a special occasion. Making up her mind, she started to type. "Thank you back," she sent and then decided since she was sending a rare text to send another. "And I'm so proud of you. Go get 'em, Tiger."

. . .

A FEW MINUTES BEFORE EIGHT, Tate confidently left her office to walk down the hall to the conference room where the most important meeting of her life was about to be held. As she turned the corner, she saw the president of the firm standing a few feet outside the doorway talking to a woman Tate did not recognize. Drawing closer, Tate could not help but notice the stranger was very attractive. Her auburn hair was pulled back from her face to fall in waves on her shoulders. A perfectly fitted black jacket over an ivory colored blouse and a matching pencil skirt hugged her body and could not help but show off the woman's shapely legs.

When Tate was closer, the pair turned as if getting ready to walk into the conference room when the president noticed Tate coming toward them. "Tate Nilsen," he said with a warm smile. "It's good to see you. I'd like to introduce you to Aurora Price." The woman turned to face Tate, and she realized the woman was even more attractive than she first thought. Piercing green eyes reflecting intelligence, but also sensuality, met her own. Full lips touched with just the right amount of maroon lipstick turned up into a smile. *Somehow the perfect blend of feminine, but exudes strength too*, Tate thought. *I wonder where she came from and why she's here.*

Aurora held out her hand. "It's a pleasure to meet you, Ms. Nilsen," she said, and Tate returned the gesture, finding the grip warm, and delicate, but not weak.

"The pleasure is mine," Tate said. "And please, you can call me Tate."

The woman raised her eyebrows. "Such an unusual name," she said with a hint of sincere curiosity. "Do you mind if I ask where it comes from?"

"I don't mind at all. It comes from Norse Mythology," Tate answered. "My father is a professor at Portland State University and has always had a sweet spot for Vikings."

"I see," Aurora said and for a moment their eyes held. For

a second, Tate felt almost mesmerized. There was a strange chemistry between them. *This woman is very charismatic*, she thought, and wondered if she would ever see her again. *I think she would be interesting to know.*

"Well, we best get in there," the president interrupted, breaking what almost felt like a spell over Tate.

"Yes, let's go," Aurora said turning on one of her heels to walk with the president into the conference room.

Tate followed, looking for an open seat in the crowded space. One of her coworkers waved her over to the empty chair beside him. "Thanks," Tate said as she checked the clock on the wall and tried to settle in. It was eight on the dot. Her heart raced with adrenaline, and she felt her palms starting to sweat. Hopefully the meeting would get straight to the point before she hyperventilated.

As if reading her mind, the president stood and held up his hands for quiet. All murmuring stopped. "Thank you all for your time this Monday morning," he said. "I know there is a lot of work to be done, but I wanted to take a moment to talk to you about teamwork." His face grew serious. "Teamwork is essential to success in this company. It is the key to completing tasks efficiently and effectively. Good teamwork can help to improve communication, increase productivity, and promote a positive work environment." The man let his eyes scan the room, and Tate couldn't help but wonder what he was getting at exactly. In her opinion, the firm worked like a well-oiled machine. Numbers had never been higher. Bonuses should be record setting that fall. *What does this have to do with my promotion?* she wondered as the man continued. "However, teamwork is not always easy. It takes effort and cooperation from all members of a team to make it work. When teamwork is not effective, it can lead to conflict, decreased productivity, and a negative work environment. And nobody wants that, right?"

For a beat no one moved, but then people's heads nodded as they realized what he said had been a real question. The president smiled. "Good," he said. "Now, with that being said, I'd like to make an official announcement."

Tate held her breath. *This has to be it,* she thought, ready to finally be rewarded for her years of hard work. "As you know, the Vice President of Mergers and Acquisitions position here has been vacant for a while," he said. "But no longer. I'd like to introduce you all to our newest VP, Aurora Price."

For a moment, Tate was sure she heard the room hush, and then for a minute nothing else registered. The urge to puke nearly overcame her, but she swallowed it down. Over the sound of her heart pounding in her ears, she knew the president was saying more. Something about needing to bring in a fresh, outside perspective to the firm and then the listing of Aurora's credentials. Finally, the woman herself stood to address the room. Unable to help it, Tate stared at her only to find her looking right back, the hint of a smile on her lips, as if they were the only two people in the room.

5

Finishing the last of her sweet pear and walnut salad and taking the plastic bowl to the recycling bin, Liza tried not to think about how horrible her morning had gone. It seemed like nothing but one complaint after another. Angry clients who were frustrated about what was and was not covered by their insurance policy. Fender benders, flooded garages, even a lost wedding ring had swamped the team of four insurance specialists working the phones. *Not a great start for the week*, she thought straightening her dress as she headed back to her building in downtown Portland. Not that she disliked her job, but being an insurance specialist in an office all day was not her lifelong dream. She liked helping people when they were polite, but she didn't like being hung up on.

Glancing at her phone and seeing that it was one-thirty and time for her to return to her desk, she was a little surprised there was nothing from Tate. When they discussed things last night, it seemed logical the announcement regarding the promotion would be sometime in the morning. That would give her time to start her transition from her old team to her new position. With no word, Liza had to assume that the official announcement had yet to happen. Still, Liza didn't worry too much. Tate was certain to get the VP job. It was more likely Tate was too busy jumping into her new role to text, even on such a special occasion.

Walking down the hallway to enter the office Liza shared with the other specialists, she waved at her coworker and friend Emma to let her know she could go on her lunch break. Liza dropped her purse in a desk drawer and took a seat. Slipping on her headset, she prepared to take the next call. While she waited, she wondered if maybe it would be a good night to call her friends together to meet at Ruby's. They didn't typically meet on Mondays, but tonight would be a special occasion. She had been dying to tell her friends about Tate's new job, and they would want to celebrate with them. But until she heard from Tate, she didn't dare make any plans. It would be too hard to explain without spilling the beans. *What about dinner with only Tate someplace special?* she thought. *I could at least make a reservation somewhere so we can have champagne and celebrate.* They hadn't made it to dinner or even out of the apartment last night and the memory of why made her cheeks flush a little. Instead, the two of them ended up ordering takeout and sat in their robes on the couch while they ate. They hadn't been so connected and laid back in a long time, and it had felt very good. *It's all because we are on the brink of a new chapter.*

Before she could make up her mind what to do the line beeped and a new call came in. "Hello. This is Barb Williams' Insurance Office. How may I help you?" she asked.

"I need to make a claim," came a gravelly voice. "Someone broke into my car last night." With a quick scan of her computer screen, Liza was able to determine who the customer was based on his phone number. He was a long-time customer with quite a few claims over the years.

Still, she confirmed. "Who am I speaking with?" she asked, and the man gave her his name. A quick look at the policy and Liza knew the conversation would not go well. The man had only the most basic liability insurance on his only vehicle. It would not cover a break in. "Sir. I'm sorry to tell you that a break in is not covered under your car insurance policy."

"What?" the man growled. "Then what do I pay you for every month?"

Patiently, Liza explained the details of his policy and the limitations. At the end, he finished the call by calling her useless, among other things, and hung up. Liza had never wanted to quit more than at that moment, but she took a few deep breaths and stayed at her desk. The time would come soon when she could permanently call it quits, and for Liza, it couldn't come soon enough.

HER DAY WAS A BLUR. Tate swung from total numbness to nausea and back as she sat through one meeting after another. Meetings that centered around Aurora Price and bringing her up to speed. For the most part, even though she was a key member of the team, Tate stayed silent, simply staring at the wooden conference table and trying to piece together what happened to her career. When she would look up to answer a direct question, the auburn-haired stranger and the firm's newest vice president seemed to always be staring at her with a little half-smile on her pretty face. If Tate had been her normal self, she might have wondered what the woman was thinking, but at the moment, all she focused on was getting through what felt like the longest day of her life.

Whenever she got the chance to scurry back to her office, close the door, and sit in her chair, all she could do was stare at her computer monitor. It was like her brain was fried by the bad news and had somehow disconnected from her body. The usual activities of her day-to-day job were forgotten. When a chime came from her laptop, Tate saw a new email had come in, adding to the growing list of unopened correspondence. It was a meeting invite, and the subject line listed Tate's three biggest accounts. With a sick feeling in her stomach, she clicked on the email only to read a short statement that said it all. She was to prepare a presentation later that evening for Aurora Price to hand over to her the accounts she had spent years cultivating a good relationship with and who were huge moneymakers. The words hit her like a punch in the gut and the nausea returned.

Looking at the time, she saw it was scheduled for seven p.m., much later than many other of the firm's employees worked. Still, she moved the mouse, letting the cursor hover over the accept button. For the last decade, she had accepted meeting requests no matter the time they were scheduled. She always made herself available, but today she couldn't force herself to click the button. *What would happen if I declined it?* she wondered. *What if I finally said no?* Slowly it dawned on her that maybe it was because she never pushed back that cost her the promotion. *Maybe they think I'm weak and too much of a sheep.*

Tears stung her eyes at the thought it might be true, and instead of clicking accept or decline, she did nothing at all. Suddenly, she had to leave. The walls of her office felt like they were closing in and grabbing her bag, she stood. She was about to do the unthinkable, but she didn't care. She was simply going to walk out. Stepping out her door she saw two colleagues talking to the executive assistant. When they noticed her, they immediately stopped talking, and Tate saw the worst thing she could imagine—pity on their faces. "I'm going to be out for the rest of the day," Tate stammered.

The executive assistant opened her mouth to respond, but before she could say a word, Tate strode to the elevators. She could not get out of there fast enough and wanted to be home where she could be alone until Liza got back. *Liza*, she thought as the elevator doors slid open and she stepped onboard. *How will I tell her?*

PULLING into her garage at home, Liza was caught off guard when she saw Tate's vehicle was already there. She couldn't remember the last time the woman was home on a workday before Liza. She had left her office at five o'clock sharp, and even with a commute, it was still incredibly early for Tate's workday to be over. *And why didn't she send a text?* Liza wondered. *If she was going to leave early, I would've asked for the time off too.* Then an idea struck her. Tate was probably planning a big surprise for Liza and waiting for her to walk through the back door. There would likely be chilled champagne ready to pop so they could toast the new chapter of their lives. Her eyes widened. *And there might even be a ring involved.*

Liza rushed into the house and paused when all the lights were off. There was nothing to greet her, not even a sound, and for the second time in two days, Liza was not sure what to think. *Her car is in the garage though*, she thought. *And I don't believe she would have gone for a run on such an important day.* There was a noise in the kitchen, and Liza walked in expectantly only to find their cat, Zombie, eating a bit of kibble. He looked up when she entered before refocusing on his bowl. "Where is Tate?" she asked him, but Zombie stayed occupied with his dinner.

Putting her purse on the kitchen counter, Liza decided that if Tate was home, there could only be two places where she was hiding. Possibly in bed waiting for her, which seemed a little unlikely after last night, however not impossible given the events of the day. *Maybe she feels especially powerful*, she thought with a tingle and started in that direction. As she did, she crossed the doorway that led into the extra bedroom they used as Tate's home office. The door was closed, which was rare unless Tate was on a call. Leaning closer, Liza paused to listen. There was nothing but silence and when she looked, she saw the room was clearly dark because she couldn't see any light seeping around the door. Still, something instinctive told her Tate was inside. For the first time, she felt a trickle of worry as she gently opened the door. "Tate?" she asked softly. There was no answer, but she sensed her partner was in the room.

Opening the door all the way, she stepped inside only to find the woman in her executive chair, turned to look out the window. Only the early evening light lit the room, casting long shadows across the walls. On the desk was a half-full bottle of bourbon. "What are you doing?" Liza asked feeling her cheeks flush with fear, disappointment, and a little anger. Something was very wrong, and she knew it.

"I want to be alone," Tate answered softly. "We can talk about everything later."

"No," Liza said, her body cold with dread. "We'll talk about it now. Tell me what happened."

Tate whirled around in her chair, fixing Liza with a stare. Even in the dim light, Liza saw Tate's face was pale, and her short hair was disheveled as if she had been running her hands through it over and over. "You want to talk about it?" Tate said in a tight voice. "Fine. Aurora Price is what happened."

Liza blinked. "Who is Aurora Price?"

"The new VP of Mergers and Acquisitions at the firm," Tate said.

Liza thought she misheard, certain they wouldn't have

given the job to someone else, especially someone she had never heard Tate mention before. "But I thought that's what you were going to be?"

Tate barked out a laugh, but there is no humor in it, only what Liza recognized was pain. "I thought that too. But I guess I'm not good enough," she answered.

Liza shook her head, tears welling up in her eyes. "Tate," she said. "How could you let this happen?"

## 6

Slowly pouring another inch of bourbon, Tate considered Liza's question. *How did I let this happen?* she wondered. *Or worse, how did I not even see it coming?* Over the top of her glass as she swallowed half of the burning liquid, she saw Lisa continuing to stare at her. The look on the woman's face was nothing but horror. "I don't have an answer for that," Tate said, and she meant it. The sense of bewilderment remained, although the numbness slowly melted from the bourbon's effects. Gradually, anger took place, something she rarely gave into, but today was going to be an exception. She had been screwed out of a position she had worked her ass off for, day and night for years. Weekends. Holidays. Anniversaries. She gave everything to the firm. A slow fire inside her started to build. *Who the hell is Aurora Price anyway?* There had to be more to the story, but it didn't take away the sense of failure.

Drinking again, she swallowed before staring into the empty glass. "I guess I just wasn't good enough," she said, and a sound, somewhere between a sob and a growl, came from Liza.

"I don't believe that," she said. "You're the best for that job. You said so yourself and promised me it would happen."

Tate's anger spilled over, and she slapped her hand on the desktop. "Stop," she said. "I never made any promises to you."

For a moment there was no sound in the room as their eyes held. A tear ran down Liza's face, but Tate saw the anger building up in Liza too. Her fiery, feisty girlfriend was about to let go a tirade. In a way, Tate welcomed it. *Maybe it's what I deserve*, she thought. *Maybe I did make it sound too certain.*

She opened her mouth to apologize, but Lisa held up an angry finger. "I don't want excuses," Lisa snapped. "Just tell me what happens now?"

At that question, Tate leaned back in her chair because she wasn't sure of the answer. She wouldn't lie. A small sliver of her wanted to quit her job and tell them to shove it. But Tate would never do that. She was responsible and trustworthy and wouldn't flush a decade of her life down the toilet because of something out of her control. If they wanted Aurora Price instead of her, there was nothing she could do about it.

Liza stomped her foot. "Answer me, God dammit."

Tate blew out a long breath, trying to buy a little time before crushing her girlfriend's hopes. "We keep doing what we're doing," she answered. "Nothing has changed."

"No," Liza shot back. "I will not accept that answer. I can't take this anymore."

Tate furrowed her brow. "What does that mean?"

Crossing her arms, Liza lifted her chin. "You know what I want," she said, her eyes smoldering. "I want to be married. I want to have a baby. We can't keep waiting forever." At the words, Tate felt her chest clench with anxiety. Liza was right. Tate had heard the same speech over and over, and although Tate always hoped it was enough to simply provide a nice home and comfortable life, it was never adequate. The woman always wanted more from her, but after what happened at work today, Tate couldn't take the thought that she failed Liza.

Standing, Tate looked hard at the woman she loved. "You're right," she said. "You shouldn't have to wait any longer. If what I give you is not enough, then…" She let the words dwindle off. As angry as she was, she wouldn't say something she couldn't take back.

Still, a look of shock crossed Liza's face as she clearly finished the sentence in her mind. "You can't mean that," she said, with anger but also hurt in her voice.

"I honestly don't know what I mean right now," Tate growled as she walked around the desk, storming out of the office. "All I know is I need another drink somewhere other than here."

FOR THE FIRST time in a very long time, Liza was speechless. She watched as her infinitely patient and steady girlfriend stormed out of her office. She heard the woman's heavy steps on the wood floor as she walked to the garage and then the slamming of the door. For a moment she thought about running after her, but then it was too late as she heard the garage door opening. Tate left in her SUV. Somehow her girlfriend's abrupt departure made her even more hurt and angry. *And don't forget disappointed*, she thought. *She had seemed so sure she would get that promotion. This doesn't make sense.*

Over the years, Tate had explained to her as patiently as possible how her line of business worked. Moving up the chain required more than skill and intelligence, it required dedication and time served. They had to put in the work and the hours that went with it. "But it will all be worth it in the end," Tate had said, and Liza had believed her. *And now this?*

she thought, storming into the kitchen to grab her phone from her purse. The desire to call Tate's boss, a man she met on a number of occasions at boring business dinners, was hard to resist. She would give him a piece of her mind and started to call Tate's firm to be connected to the man's office, but then hesitated. Tate would likely never forgive her for something so reckless. *And maybe this is all just a big mistake.*

Her next thought was to text Tate and tell her she needed to come home so they could discuss things further. There had to be a way to still get the promotion she was promised. But a part of her knew that in the rare times Tate became angry, it was best to let the woman cool off somewhere on her own. Give her a little space. *But I'm not going to just sit here*, she thought and called Allie. "Hi, Liza," Allie answered in her usual cheerful voice.

"Hi. What are you doing?" Liza snapped, and then caught herself. None of what happened was her friend's fault. "Sorry, I was wondering what you were doing tonight."

There was a pause of hesitation and in the background Liza heard the din of other voices. "I'm actually at Ruby's," Allie answered. "With Vivian and Nikki. We were talking about the upcoming Portland Pride Festival and what Ruby's might do with the booth we rented."

"I see," was all Liza could think to say, a little disappointed.

"But I can come over if you need me to," Allie quickly added. For a moment Liza considered taking her friend up on her offer but then realized there had been far too many nights over the last year where Allie had come to her rescue when she was frustrated with Tate working late. It wasn't fair to pull her friend away from something important.

"No," Liza finally said. "This can wait."

"Are you sure?"

"I'm sure," Liza lied.

"You can always come to Ruby's," Allie added. "We could use your creative ideas." Liza cocked her head as she thought about her friend's offer. Any minute now Tate would probably walk through the bar's front door, and the truth would be out that they were having another fight. The last thing she wanted was to take out her frustrations on Tate amongst her friends. Again.

Liza sighed. "I think I'll just stay home," she answered. "I have some online shopping I want to catch up on."

"Okay, but if you change your mind, send me a text," Allie said and Liza nodded.

"I will. Good luck with your planning."

"Thank you," Allie said, and they disconnected. Looking around the empty house, Liza blew out an angry breath. A storm was building inside her and she didn't know what to do about it. The urge to throw something was strong, and she eyeballed the bouquet of flowers Tate had given her. They almost seemed to mock her, but a sliver of reason kept her from flinging the whole thing at the wall. With no other outlet, Liza let out a scream of absolute frustration before throwing herself on one of the couches. It seemed she would be alone waiting for Tate after all.

CIRCLING the block for the third time, Tate grew more and more frustrated when she couldn't find a parking spot on a street anywhere near Ruby's. As heavy summer rain started to patter the windshield, she finally squeezed her Explorer into a spot three blocks away. *How appropriate*, she thought as she got out and realized she had not picked up her coat when she stormed out of the house. *Maybe a walk in the pouring rain will do me good*.

By the time she reached Ruby's front door, the sky had opened its floodgates. Her short hair was plastered to her head, her clothes looked like she had worn them in a shower, and water ran down her face. Walking inside, she noticed Vivian and Allie standing with Nikki at the bar counter. The three women were deep in conversation, at least until they noticed her. She couldn't miss the look that passed among them as they took in her appearance and sudden arrival.

"Well, now," Nikki drawled. "You look a little bit like a drowned rat. Everything okay, Tate?"

"No," Tate snapped as she took a seat on the stool beside her best friend. "Nothing is okay." Out of the corner of her eye she saw Allie slip away toward Vivian's office. It was likely the woman was going to grab her coat and then disappear out the back door en route to check on Liza. *Funny how she didn't even have to ask a question to think that we were fighting again*, Tate thought with a bit of sadness. *Are we that bad?* Then it dawned on her Liza might have already reached out and told her friends what was going on. *Well, at least Liza will have someone to vent to about my failures.*

"What can I get you?" Vivian asked from the other side of the bar. "Bourbon on the rocks?"

"Yes, please," Tate said trying to rein in her anger. It was completely unlike her, and she shouldn't direct her frustration at her friends. They weren't the ones who stole her promotion.

Vivian nodded. "Coming up."

While Vivian pulled a bottle from the top shelf of the rows behind her, Nikki leaned in. "I'm a little confused," her friend said quietly. "You were on cloud nine yesterday at the gym and now you look ready to commit murder. What the hell happened?"

Tate sucked in a deep breath and slowly let it out. "I didn't tell you because I didn't want to jinx it," Tate finally answered, unable to help but see the irony of the situation. She had been careful, but it didn't help. "But I was up for a big promotion at work. So big that it would change mine and Liza's life forever."

"And?" Nikki asked with a raised eyebrow. "Doesn't take a rocket scientist to figure out something went wrong there."

Take shook her head. "No, it doesn't," she said. "I didn't get the promotion. They gave it to another woman who I've never even seen before."

Vivian set the glass of bourbon in front of Tate while Nikki let out a long whistle. "An outsider," she said. "Wow."

"Yeah, wow," Tate added as she reached for her wallet.

Vivian waved her off. "That one's on the house."

"Thank you," Tate said and Vivian nodded.

"That's tough luck," she said. "I haven't known you for that long, but I can tell you work hard for that company, and you deserve to be treated better."

Tate felt the sting of tears. What Vivian said was true—she did deserve to be treated better. *So, now what?* she wondered, picking up her drink. *And what do I do about Aurora Price?*

## 7

When there was a quiet knock at the front door, Liza didn't have to think twice to know who was outside—Allie. If Allie was still at Ruby's when an angry Tate arrived, it was likely she correctly guessed Liza was upset and so came over for support. *That's why I love her so much*, Liza thought, opening the door. "You're right on time," she said. "I just opened a fresh bottle of red."

"Sounds perfect," Allie said as she walked in from the rain. "This weather is impossible." After taking off her damp coat, Allie hung it on the rack near the door a moment before opening her arms. Liza stepped in for a reassuring hug. It felt good to have someone care so much, and they stood there for a moment before Liza pulled back, quickly wiping a tear from her eye.

"So, let me guess," Liza said, gathering herself as she led the way to the kitchen. "My phone call plus Tate probably showing up at the bar was enough for you to figure out we had had another fight."

Allie gave her a sad smile. "Yes," she said. "It was impossible to miss. But I will say Tate looked terrible." Liza felt a stab of guilt in her chest. Her girlfriend had a horrible day at work with the bad news, yet Liza piled on because of her own hurt and disappointment. *Which was unfair to her*, Liza thought as she poured the second glass of wine. *But I can't seem to help myself. I lash out when I'm hurt, disappointed, or especially when I'm scared.* The sudden turn of events did scare her. She didn't know how it would affect her future with Tate.

Handing the wine to Allie she sighed. "Did you hear anything about what happened?" she asked as Allie took the glass.

"I slipped away as soon as I saw her so upset."

"I see," Liza said wondering for a second if it was finally okay to tell people about Tate's promised promotion. *Oh, what the hell*, she thought. *It's not like things can get more screwed up than they already are.* "Well, remember how I was excited about looking at engagement rings yesterday?"

"Yes," Allie said with a raised eyebrow. "Please don't tell me this is about a proposal gone wrong."

Leading them to the couch, Liza sat. "Not exactly," she said. "It's not like she proposed or something but rather I had hoped she would propose because she was going to get a big promotion at work." Liza felt a hard stab of disappointment and a fresh burn of tears. "But then she didn't get the promotion, so no proposal."

"I'm so sorry," Allie said lowered herself to the spot beside Liza. "That must be devastating for both of you."

"It is," Liza said after taking a sip. "But of course, I dealt with it badly. I flew off the handle and threw the fact that I wanted to be married and have a baby in Tate's face yet again." She shook her head. "So, she left."

.

. . .

"Okay, what's the plan?" Nikki asked from where she sat on her stool beside her friend.

Tate wasn't sure what she meant. "Plan?" she asked. "You mean other than sit here and get wasted?"

Nikki shook her head with a grim smile. "Although I always consider that a solution to many of life's problems, I think in this case we need to brainstorm a little bit instead."

Standing behind the bar across from them, Vivian held her own drink. "In this case, even though I own the bar and sell the alcohol, I have to agree," she said, with a hint of a smile. "If this situation is as big a surprise to you as it appears, maybe there's something you can do about it."

Tate rubbed her face with her hands to try and clear the cobwebs from the bourbon. *How do I explain this?* she thought. Her friends meant well, but they didn't work in the world of corporate business. They clearly didn't understand the hierarchical structure of things. People were passed over from time to time, even when it didn't make sense. *Or it did if they simply didn't cut it.* Once again, a sense of inferiority rocked her. *Is that what this is? Am I blind to my own shortcomings?*

Clearly, the firm thought bringing in an outsider was a better option than making her the VP. "I think I'll just have to keep my head down and hope for the best," Tate finally said quietly.

"Oh, come on," Nikki said as she fixed Tate with a hard look. "That is not the person you are, so there's more to this than you're telling." She leaned closer until Tate was forced to look at her. "I need more details as to why you think you shouldn't fight this."

"Sorry," Tate started. "But I don't really have answers for you. The woman they brought in is named Aurora Price." Even saying the woman's name stung. "Aside from what I managed to hear through the daze I was in after the announcement she was taking my promotion, I know nothing about her."

She saw Vivian take out her phone. "Did you say her name was Aurora Price?" she asked. Tate nodded and watched the woman type. After a beat Vivian tilted her head. "Well, she certainly has some creds, on paper. There's a lengthy list of her accomplishments on Google."

"Let me see," Nikki said, holding out her hand. Vivian passed her the phone, and Tate watched Nikki's eyes widen. "Not to mention she's a real looker." Tate smiled a little at the comment. Leave it to her best friend to find something sexy about the direst of circumstances. "But it says she's a big deal in Chicago, so why the hell is she in Portland?"

"It's a beautiful place to live?" Tate asked.

Nikki hummed. "It seems a little off to me," she said. "I'm going back to my original statement; you shouldn't take this lying down." Tate looked at her friends and felt a little confidence returning. *Maybe they are right,* she thought, but before she could say a word, her own phone chimed.

When she looked at the screen, there was a text from Liza. "I'm sorry. Please come home so we can talk." Tate hesitated, not sure she was ready to move past everything, when another text from Liza came. The message surprised her a little. "I know this wasn't your fault, and I promise to listen." Reading the words, feeling the support of everyone, Tate realized if they believed in her then maybe she was underestimating herself. She deserved the position, and if she always stood up for her clients, maybe it was time to stand up for herself.

As SHE WAITED on the couch with Allie, Liza began to feel uneasy. Tate had yet to send back a response to her text. *Is she that angry with me?* she wondered, feeling her own frustration grow again. After all, she had been the one to put out the olive branch, hoping they could move past the hurtful words. *But if she's not willing to even talk to me about it, then what?*

Suddenly there is a sharp knock at the front door. "Are you expecting someone tonight?" Allie asked, eyebrows raised. "Other than Tate I mean?"

"No, and I don't know why she would come to the front door," Liza replied as she stood and moved toward the window to peek outside through the curtains. A man in a black coat stood on the steps getting wet in the rain. Although it was dark with the porch light still off, she was pretty sure it wasn't someone she recognized. In a beat, Allie was at her side, right as the man knocked again. "Should I open it?" Liza whispered, not a big fan of opening doors to strangers, especially after dark.

Allie looked uncertain. "Maybe wait for Tate?"

Unfortunately, Liza didn't know when that might be and the annoyance over not knowing spurred her on. "I'm going to see who it is," she said, flipping on the porch light as she moved to the door and opened it a crack. "May I help you?"

The man held up two brown paper sacks marked with the name of the closest Mexican restaurant. "Someone named Tate ordered dinner," the man said, and Liza let out a breath. *Leave it to Tate to think about taking care of dinner,* she thought. *She must be on her way home.*

At that moment she heard the back door to the garage opening. "Well, hi you two," she heard Allie say while Liza took the two sacks and nudged the door closed with her hip. Turning, she wasn't surprised to see it was Nikki with Tate. The two always had each other's back, and she was grateful for it tonight.

Tate crossed the space, reaching for the bags and leaning in to give Liza a peck on the lips. "Sorry to not call or text," she said. "My phone's battery died right after I ordered us dinner. It's been that kind of day."

Liza smelled the bourbon on her girlfriend's breath and wondered how many drinks she had ended up having. *Getting drunk is not going to fix this but at least she didn't drive home intoxicated,* she thought. *A DUI is the last thing we need.* "Okay," was all she could come up with and, for a moment, there was an awkward silence in the room.

"I thought I'd be the chauffeur," Nikki said with a smile, always one to break a silence. "So, I drove Tate home in her car." She looked at Allie. "Hoping that you were still here. I don't suppose you can give me a ride back to Ruby's?"

"Of course," Allie said moving toward the coat rack. "I think it's time to go anyway."

Suddenly, Liza wasn't sure she was ready to be alone with Tate and deal with their problems. "Are you sure you don't want to stay and have some takeout with us?"

Allie gave Liza a quick side hug. "Not this time," she said and whispered into Liza's ear. "I think you two need to talk." She slipped on her coat and led Nikki toward the way out. "I'll text you tomorrow."

Then they were gone, and Liza was alone with Tate. The two stared at each other for a long moment, not moving. Finally, Tate set the two bags of food on the coffee table and opened her arms. Liza went to her. "I'm sorry," they said in unison, which resulted in a tentative laugh from each. "I promise to be more patient this time," Liza said. "But I need to understand exactly what happened."

Tate sighed, and gently pulled away. "It's like I said," she replied, picking up the food and walking toward the kitchen. "They brought in an outsider named Aurora Price."

"But who the hell is that?" Liza asked, trailing behind her.

With a shake of her head, Tate gathered plates and silverware. "Nobody is sure," she answered. "Vivian looked her up online. She's some bigwig from Chicago. I don't know why they think she's qualified to be the VP of Mergers and Acquisitions here in Portland." Liza frowned. Nothing added up. They had been so sure Tate would get the promotion only to have it pulled away at the last second. *For someone else?* she wondered. *That we haven't even heard of?*

Opening the bags and pulling out packages of food, Liza wasn't sure how to ask her next question without sounding argumentative, but she had to know. "Tate, what will you do about it?" she asked, and Tate paused.

"Nikki thinks I should fight it," she replied.

"And will you?"

After a moment of hesitation Tate nodded. "Yes, I'll talk to my boss tomorrow morning and get to the bottom of this."

8

Tate arrived at work earlier than normal for two reasons. First, being unable to sleep because of the nerves she felt about confronting her boss and second, the desire to get a jump on the work she missed by leaving early the day before. Regardless of the outcome from her discussion with her boss, she had a feeling Aurora Price would not be going anywhere anytime soon. If that was the case, she would need to give the presentation regarding Tate's three biggest clients. Always professional, she would take the time to develop some slides with statistics and key information. She owed it to her clients even if she didn't owe it to the woman who took her promotion.

As she exited the elevator onto her office's floor, she noticed some of the main lights already on. Sometimes the cleaning crew forgot to shut everything off, so she didn't think much of it as she dropped her laptop bag off in her office. Yet when she went to the floor's breakroom where they had a refrigerator, some round tables, and a coffee maker, she noticed there was a pot of coffee already made. *Okay,* she thought. *I am definitely not alone here.* Curious, she made her way down the hall until she realized the office with the lights on was the one that used to belong to the VP of Mergers and Acquisitions. The reminder of what she lost made her grit her teeth. *What would have been my new office.* She didn't have to guess it was more than likely the person inside the room was Aurora Price. *And I have nothing to say to her.*

Starting to turn back toward the breakroom and grab some coffee, she hesitated. Having animosity with the new vice president would not be in her best interest, especially if the woman didn't know the impact she had on Tate's life. *Maybe Aurora doesn't even realize,* she thought. *And in that case, I can't hold any of this against her personally.* Tate should at least be cordial. Taking a deep breath, she turned again and went to the open office door. As she suspected, Aurora sat at the desk along the floor-to-ceiling windows of the executive office. Her auburn-haired head was bent as she studied some papers on her desk. Again, Tate hesitated. She simply wasn't sure if she was ready to start a conversation with the woman.

Before she could make up her mind, Aurora seemed to sense Tate was in the doorway and looked up. "Oh," she said clearly startled to see someone standing in the there. "I didn't know anyone would be here yet."

Tate shrugged. "I decided I needed to be here early today."

"And why is that?" Aurora asked. "Is there something I should know about?"

For a moment, Tate thought about being vague with her answer. The new VP didn't need to know everything she was doing, but then she took a deep breath. "It's about the three clients that I am supposed to brief you on," she said. "I want to make sure I'm prepared for our meeting."

Aurora leaned back in her chair and steepled her fingers. "I see," she said. "You did do a vanishing act yesterday from what I hear. I hope everything is okay."

"Everything is fine. Something came up," Tate said, then took a step back. "Well, I won't bother you any longer. I just wanted to see why the light was on."

"Wait," Aurora said before Tate could walk away. "Since you're here and I'm here, maybe we should get to know each other better. Come in and tell me a little about yourself." She waved toward the chair opposite her desk. "After all were going to be working closely together."

WALKING along the city sidewalk in the direction of her favorite little coffee shop, Liza was glad the rain from the day before had finally stopped. She found nothing more depressing than rain in June. Portland had more than enough during the months between October and April. The summer was meant to be clear and beautiful, and luckily, the day was starting off that way. Blue skies with a warm, gentle breeze on her face felt good. *Maybe it's a sign that today will be a good day,* she thought. *And Tate's meeting with her boss will go well.* Nothing would make her happier if they could somehow get back to how things were even two days before.

As she reached the coffee shop door, she saw Rey through the window. Her friend was already sitting at one of the small wooden tables along the wall, looking at her phone. After all the drama from the night before, Liza was glad her friend was able to meet her before the workday started. Rey was a perfect listener and always a calming influence. When Liza woke to find Tate already gone that morning, she realized she needed to talk to someone. Pushing through the door, there was a little tinkle of bells and Rey looked over. A smile brightened her face as soon as she saw Liza walking toward her. "Am I late?" Liza asked as she navigated around the few occupied tables in the small room.

Standing, Rey shook her head before giving Liza a hug.

"Not a bit," she answered. "I was a little early and had plenty of emails to read through while I waited."

"From your new job at the nonprofit?" Liza asked as she took a seat opposite Rey.

Her friend nodded as she sat. "They keep me busy, but I could not be happier," she said. "The change has done me good."

Liza smiled a little. "I love hearing that," she said. "You deserve to be happy."

Rey tilted her head at the melancholy tone Liza had been unable to keep out of her voice. Her eyes scanned Liza's face. "I think we all deserve to be happy," she said. "How are you?"

Studying her friend's face, Liza wasn't sure how much Allie had already told Rey. "I'm okay, I think," Liza answered. "Although last night was very disappointing. Actually, that's an understatement. It was horrible."

Before she could say more, the barista called Rey's name. "I ordered you your usual—a vanilla latte. I hope that's okay," Rey said as she started away from the table.

"Of course," Liza said. "Thank you."

Watching Rey retrieve the drinks, Liza thought about how much her friend had blossomed over the last few months. She and Marty were perfect for each other, and it showed. *Are Tate and I perfect for each other?* she wondered suddenly. *Does Tate love me as much as Marty and Rey appear to love each other?* Feeling a stab of guilt at even doubting Tate's love for her, Liza was glad when Rey came back and handed her the latte.

"So, talk to me," Rey said, clearly not ready to let her earlier question drop. "Is something wrong between you and Tate?"

The question was a good one, and Liza wasn't sure how to answer it. *Is her not getting promoted really Tate's fault?* she thought, biting her lip. *Or am I being entirely unfair?* Liza sighed. "Unfortunately, yes," she answered. "There sort of is." Then, after a sip of the hot drink, she filled her friend in on the events of the night before including Tate not getting the promotion and then storming out. "And the worst thing, in my mind, is the fact that I don't think she will propose to me now."

"I see," Rey said, gently. "And I know that's important to you."

"More so every day," Liza said. "With my birthday coming it's all I can think about. My damn ticking clock."

Rey reached across the table and touched Liza's arm. "I know Tate loves you," she said. "I know she wants to make you happy."

Feeling the sting of tears at her friend's honest words, Liza sighed. "I know too," she said. "But sometimes I worry we just don't want the same thing."

CONFLICTED, Tate paused in the doorway of the office that should have been hers. She had legitimate work to do so she could say no, however, it was hard to resist an opportunity to learn more about Aurora Price. *Maybe find out why she left Chicago*, Tate thought. *And why she ended up here in the job I wanted.* "All right," Tate said. "But I only have a few minutes."

Aurora smiled. "Totally understand," she said. "I know you are busy woman." Although Tate couldn't be sure, Aurora didn't come across as completely sincere in her comment, and Tate felt her neck grow warm. *Was this the reason why I didn't get the promotion?* she wondered. *Because they don't think I work hard enough? Or is she just trying to get under my skin for some reason?* Not sure how to comment, Tate didn't respond as she stepped into the office and started for the chair.

Before she went far, Aurora held up a hand to pause her.

"Why don't you close the door," she said with a half-smile on her face that made Tate pause. Things felt odd, but she shook it off. *What harm is there in shutting the door?* she wondered and after a beat, she did as a woman asked. "Perfect. Thank you. I don't want us to be interrupted."

Still not sure what game Aurora was playing, Tate nodded as she sat in the chair. "No problem," she said and waited to see what the woman would say next.

Aurora leaned back in her expensive leather executive's chair. "So, tell me how long you've been working here."

Tate hesitated. *Does she truly not know anything about my history with the firm?* she wondered. *Could she truly not know that she bumped me out of my promotion?* Tate's mind ran through all the possibilities. *Maybe I really have totally misjudged her.* "I started here as an intern," Tate said. "In my last year of college. They hired me once I graduated, and I've been working for them ever since."

"I see," Aurora said steepling her fingers. "That is a lot of dedication. No wonder you were allowed to handle such big clients."

The way Aurora said the word *allowed* made Tate bristle. "Yes, I suppose so," Tate said, keeping her tone cool. "Their assets have grown over forty percent since I started working with them." She sat up straighter. "I consider them more than just clients but actually friends."

"Friends? Interesting," Aurora said, tilting her head as if to appraise Tate more closely. "Do you have a lot of friends, Tate?"

"Some," Tate answered not sure where the conversation was going. For a moment the comment hung in the air. Finally, Aurora leaned forward and put her elbows on the desk looking Tate in the eye. For moment, Tate could not help but see how beautiful the woman was. *Seductive*, Tate thought. *That's a better word.*

Slowly, a smile lit up the woman's face. "So perhaps we could be friends," Aurora said. It wasn't a question, and in a tone that almost bordered on… *Sultry? No, I imagined that. I am reading something weird into this. Aren't I?* Tate wondered. *What the hell is going on here?*

A little bewildered, but not willing to be intimidated, Tate did not break the woman's gaze. "Well, anything is possible I suppose," she said. "But if we are going to know each other better, maybe you can explain why you left Chicago and how you ended up in Portland?"

The smile on Aurora's face vanished and her eyes narrowed. "That's a rather direct thing to ask," Aurora said, clearly not liking the turn of the tables. "And interesting that you know I used to live in Chicago."

Tate shrugged. "I won't lie," she said. "When you arrived here so unexpectedly, I googled you."

An awkward moment passed before Aurora nodded slowly. "I see," she said. "But I think you're right, this is not a good time to chat since we are both so busy." When the woman picked up a document from the desktop and focused on it, Tate realized she was dismissed.

Clenching her jaw, Tate stood. "I agree," she said and strode to the door.

As she opened it, Aurora called from behind her. "I hope this doesn't mean we can't be friends," she said, and Tate glanced over her shoulder.

The half-smile was back on Aurora's face, and Tate had no idea what to think. The woman was the VP of Mergers and Acquisitions and held considerable power. Although not directly Tate's boss, she did have to answer to her. "Not at all," Tate said, forcing a smile. "We can certainly be friends."

9

───

As Liza wrapped up her morning at the insurance office, she was surprised to get a text from Tate. Glancing at the message, she couldn't help but feel her heart melt a little. "Sorry for storming out last night," the text said. "I love you." Liza sighed. For most people the text wouldn't be that significant, however, she knew her partner rarely sent messages during the workday. In fact, she was poor about texting a general, so the effort that had gone into her thinking of Liza and then sending a message was huge.

Quickly writing back, Liza typed, "I'm sorry too. And I love you more." There was a long pause, and Liza was about to slip her phone back in her purse guessing Tate wouldn't reply when she felt it vibrate in her hand.

Looking at the phone she actually laughed at the message. "No, I love you more." and there was a smiley face with hearts for eyes. Feeling better than she had all day, Liza thought about sending another message back but hesitated. She wasn't sure if she should press her luck.

Finally, she was brave and typed out a message. "Does this mean you will be home in time for dinner tonight?"

"I will be," Tate responded right away. "I promise." Smiling, Liza suddenly had the idea to make something special for them to eat for dinner. Tate loved chicken Parmesan over angel hair pasta, and Liza was good at making it.

All she needed was some fresh ingredients, so she turned to her workmate, Emma. "Will you cover for me?" she asked. "I want to go to the grocery store next door and grab some stuff for dinner."

"Of course," her coworker said with a smile. "And just so you know, you're absolutely glowing with excitement. Something happen?"

"Sort of," Liza said, smiling back and grabbing her purse she headed for the door. "I'll just be a few minutes."

Taking a cart from the queue when she stepped through the sliding doors into the supermarket, she moved toward the first aisle when she saw movement out of the corner of her eye. Glancing over, she was surprised to see an old college friend. "Liza?" the woman asked, and Liza paused as she took in the woman's appearance—disheveled and honestly a little tired. Liza quickly chalked up how she looked with the fact she had a toddler in the seat of the shopping cart and a baby in a sling around her body.

"My goodness, Anna," Liza said moving closer. "How long has it been? I haven't seen you in forever."

"I know," Anna said, waving a hand at the children. "I've been a little busy. But how are you?"

Liza paused, not sure how to answer. Unlike her friend who had married right out of college and was clearly productive in the baby department, Liza had done almost nothing. "Oh, you know," Liza said. "Living the best life."

Anna sighed. "That sounds wonderful," she said. "No kiddos to hold you back?"

The question stabbed Liza through the heart, but she

forced herself to keep a smile on her face. "Not just yet," she answered. "I'm not even married."

"You are so lucky," the friend gushed and then seemed to catch herself. "Not that I'm unhappy with my husband and these little ones, but sometimes I envy people who are smart enough to wait." Anna gave a little laugh. "They take away your freedom."

Liza tilted her head. *Is that what Tate is afraid of?* she wondered. *That marrying me and having a baby will take away her freedom?* She had never asked what truly made Tate unwilling to sit down and have an honest discussion about it. If she was honest with herself, she simply wasn't sure why Tate was so hesitant, other than maybe because of money. *But we can't always wait for that. Maybe tonight, over a nice dinner, we can finally talk about it.*

AFTER HAVING A DIFFICULT DAY, by four o'clock in the afternoon Tate was convinced her boss, Chad, was ducking her phone calls and not answering her emails. The man was busy, and she understood that, but she also considered him more than just her boss. Of course, they weren't buddies necessarily, but normally they chatted at least once a day and not always about work. It was confusing when he didn't make time for her. If she had to guess, he felt somewhat responsible for letting Tate get ambushed with the news her promotion was given to someone else. Although the president of the firm would have made the final decision, Chad would have at least known things had changed.

Going to his office, she would try one more time to see if she could have a short meeting with him in person. She didn't plan to start an argument or throw a fit over the change in circumstances. Since the day before, she calmed down significantly, but she still wanted some answers. Stopping outside his office, she smiled at his executive assistant. "Any chance that Chad is in?" Tate asked, and the young man averted his gaze, making himself look busy with something on the computer screen.

"Not at the moment," he said without even looking at Tate. "He's had a very busy day."

Getting a sense that the assistant was not being honest with her, Tate frowned. "I'm aware of that," she said. "But I only need a minute."

Finally looking at her, the assistant shook his head. "You'll just have to try some other time," he said so dismissively Tate wasn't sure how to react. It wasn't like Tate didn't have seniority at the firm and warranted more respect, but the cloak and dagger feel she was getting around the VP job being given to Aurora Price was making her uneasy. Things were simply not adding up.

"All right, I guess I'll check back later," Tate said, starting to turn on her heel when a thought struck her. She looked at the executive assistant. "He will be there for my four fifteen meeting to discuss my three biggest clients, won't he? The one to bring the new hire up to speed?"

"Oh yes," the young man said. "He still has that blocked off on his schedule."

"Good," Tate said. "I guess I'll see him in a few minutes then." Walking toward the conference room where the meeting was supposed to be held, she saw through the glass wall that Chad was indeed in the conference room deep in conversation with Aurora. Surprisingly, there was no one else in the room even though Tate had invited a few others. She felt it was beneficial to include a few junior associates if she was handing things off, to help them gain experience and a better understanding of how things were set up at the firm. Apparently, Chad had dismissed them for some reason.

*Because he wants to keep this meeting private?* she wondered. *But why?*

"Well, hello, Tate," Chad said when she walked in and set her laptop at the end of the table.

She quickly attached the cable to the projector. "Crazy day, Chad?" she asked, unable to keep the irritation out of her voice. Her boss smiled, but it didn't look as warm and friendly as she remembered. If anything, he looked a little sheepish.

"It has been," he answered. "But I'm glad we're all here now. Let's get this going."

"No problem," Tate replied as she brought up the PowerPoint slides and projected onto the screen. "I think this will take us less than an hour."

Aurora lifted an eyebrow. "That seems quick," she said. "I don't want you to leave anything out."

"I believe I have a thorough deck of information here, but we can certainly do a Q&A afterwards."

"Fair enough," Aurora said, leaning back in her chair but not taking her eyes off Tate's. For a second Tate thought she saw a flicker of something in them but wasn't quite sure what it meant. Then it struck her—blatant attraction. *Am I going crazy?* she wondered. *What the hell is going on here?*

Clearing her throat, she refocused on the laptop and clicked through to the first slide. "As you can see—"

Before she was able to go any further, there was a knock on the conference room door, and Chad's executive assistant poked his head in. "I'm sorry to interrupt but there's an urgent call for you, sir. The Matthew's estate?"

"Good, I've been expecting that one," Chad said standing. "I'm sorry but I have to leave this to the two of you to work out."

"But…" Tate started, feeling an unusual sense of panic. "We can reschedule."

Chad waved a hand dismissively. "Not necessary," Chad said as he went out the door, leaving Tate alone with Aurora Price.

THE TABLE WAS SET, the wine was open, and even though dinner was still in the oven staying warm, Liza knew the chicken was drying out. A quick look at the clock in the kitchen and Liza frowned. It was well past seven when Tate had been due at five. Out of frustration, Liza had sent multiple texts to Tate asking her if she was all right. As was the woman's usual style, she had not replied.

With an angry shake of her head, Liza picked up the wine sitting open on the counter and filled a wine glass. It was a healthy serving, but she was done waiting on Tate. At least as far as the drinking part. *Where the hell is she?* Liza thought as she took a long sip. It made no sense that she not only said she would be home for dinner but promised to be home. That she did not show up was infuriating. A small worm of doubt crept into her stomach. The time had come to contact Nikki and see if she knew where Tate might be. She hated to involve any of their friends, but if there had been an accident or something, she needed to know.

Picking up her phone, Liza typed a message. "Hi," she wrote. "You wouldn't happen to know where Tate is would you?" Three dots started to show that she was replying almost immediately, and for a second Liza was amazed with how quickly her friend always responded. It was especially the case considering she was one of the busiest people Liza knew. *Or at least busy with women*, Liza thought, not that she held anything against Nikki for her habit of interchanging young ladies regularly. Being a player was a strange part of the woman's charm.

The text came through. "Let me do some checking."

"Thank you," Liza wrote back, feeling a tightness in her chest over her concern for Tate. She decided to send another text to Tate. "Where are you?"

There was no response for a full minute and then she saw that Tate was writing back. "At the office but leaving now."

"What?" Liza shot back her worry turning to anger in a heartbeat. "What happened to being home for dinner?"

"We will talk about it when I get there."

Liza shook her head. Enough was enough. "I can't take this anymore," she wrote and as soon as she hit send, she realized what she had said. It was not something she wanted to admit, especially in a text to Tate, but now that it was out, she knew it was the truth.

There was a long pause. "I'll be home soon," Tate sent.

Liza put her phone onto the counter. "And she just assumes I'll be here waiting?" Liza said to the empty kitchen. *Maybe leaving for a night or two is what it would take to let Tate know I am serious,* she thought. *And she'll stop taking me for granted.*

10

After pulling into the garage and shutting the door, Tate turned off the engine but did not immediately get out of the car. A strong part of her wanted to simply turn around and go anywhere else. *Maybe I should stop in at Ruby's*, she thought. *Have a drink before dealing with everything.* Surely at least one of their friends would be there and it would give her a chance to maybe talk some things over. A chance for her to gather herself after a horrible day. She had no doubt Liza was inside the house furiously waiting for her. Tate had no trouble imaging the way Liza would act—angry, hurt, fed up.

Glancing at her phone, she saw the multiple texts from her girlfriend each one escalating. Except the last one which made Tate realize she had worried the woman she loved. Still, she hadn't known what to say to explain and so she hadn't sent anything. Texting was never her thing. She was more of a face-to-face kind of person, which she knew often frustrated Liza.

With a deep sigh, Tate was about to get out of the SUV when her cell phone buzzed again. If Liza was still home, she would've heard the garage door open, so it was possible the text was not from her. *Unless she's going to ask me why I'm just sitting here*, Tate thought as she looked at the screen and saw a message from Nikki. "Hey. Where are you? People are getting a little worried." Tate felt even worse. Apparently, Liza had called in reinforcements when she couldn't reach her. *So now I've worried even more people I care about.*

She shot back a quick response. "Just pulled into the garage," she typed. "Nothing to worry about." With that she prepared to face the music and got out of the car to let herself into her house. As she suspected, most of the lights were off, including the dining room which was now likely set for a nice dinner. Wandering further into the house, she stopped in the living room and saw Liza on the couch. She was holding a glass of wine and at first would not meet Tate's eyes.

Not knowing what to say Tate stood there silently until finally her girlfriend gave her a glare. "Where have you been?" Liza asked. "I was worried when you didn't answer my texts."

"I'm sorry," Tate said. "I ended up having to work late to bring the new VP up to speed."

Liza gave a slow nod. "So, does that mean you didn't talk to your boss about the situation?"

"I didn't get a chance."

Narrowing her eyes, Liza fixed Tate with a look. "Is there something else I should know about the situation? Maybe you should tell me more about this VP?" At that Tate held her breath. The last thing she wanted to talk about was Aurora Price and how their evening together had gone.

The meeting had been rocky with Aurora asking questions of all kinds, and not just about the three big clients which were supposed to be the focus of the presentation. Aurora had interrupted early on with a question that caught

Tate off guard. "You're not wearing a ring," she had said with a raised eyebrow. "Does that mean you're single?"

Tate had frozen, not even sure how to respond to such an inappropriate question. "No, I'm not," Tate finally said keeping her voice calm. "I have a girlfriend." Aurora had nodded but there was a sly smile on her face. Then the woman had redirected them back on topic at hand with a work-related question. Being jerked around had knocked Tate off balance, yet somehow, they muddled through. The one-hour presentation took three hours. She thought it was probably Aurora's intention all along.

"You've taken a long time to answer," Liza said. "Was that a hard question?"

"There's nothing to say," Tate said. "And I can see this is not a good time to try to have a conversation." She set her bag on the couch and started to unbutton the top of her shirt. "I'm going to take a shower."

"Maybe you should do that," Liza snapped. "I'm so angry I'm not even sure I know what to say."

With that Tate turned, not bothering to say another word, and retreated to the bathroom.

SITTING ON THE COUCH, wine glass still in her hand, Liza wasn't lying when she said she didn't know what to say. She had been angry many times in their relationship, but it had always been rather superficial. Even when it was over topics like marriage and children, she never worried too deeply that their relationship was in trouble. But for the first time, she did worry. They seemed to be racing toward a crossroads, and she didn't know what it meant. A part of her wanted to go into the bedroom and confront Tate. She wanted to find a way to reassure herself that everything was still okay, and yet even in her anger and frustration, she knew it would not be welcome. Her usually stoic girlfriend wouldn't talk about anything serious until she was ready, and that could take hours if not days.

Liza's cell phone on the coffee table rattled with the vibration of a text coming in. She took a quick glance at the screen and saw it was Nikki. Although the timing wasn't perfect, she knew Nikki would mean well, so she decided to read the text. "Everyone home okay?" the message said. There wasn't an easy way to answer the question, especially in a text so Liza decided to call her friend. "Hey there," Nikki said after one ring. "Are you okay?"

"I'm not sure," Liza said, filled with emotion. Tears burned her eyes. "Things are crazy here."

"Like crazy fighting?"

Liza thought about what Nikki asked. *Are we really even fighting?* she wondered. *Or am I just mad and upset.* "I'm not really sure, which is almost more frightening," Liza answered. "Tate's in the shower. She didn't want to talk anymore after I asked her about her new coworker."

"Ah, the mysterious Aurora Price," Nikki said.

Sitting up straighter on the couch, Liza didn't like the way Nikki said the woman's name. "Yes, I think that's her," Liza asked. "Is there something I should know?"

Nikki paused for a beat. "I don't think so," Nikki said. "But things do seem weird about her arrival in Portland and taking over the promotion Tate was expecting."

"She's not from Portland?"

"No, Google said she was from Chicago. A pretty big name, so it doesn't make sense she would make a sudden change," Nikki replied. "I think I'll dig a little deeper."

Feeling relieved to hear Nikki would look into things, she was about to thank her when Tate's phone started ringing in her bag on the couch. Liza wanted very much to see who was calling. "I need to go," Liza said. "I'll reach out to you later."

"Okay," Nikki said a moment before the call disconnected. Liza scrambled to the other couch and fished Tate's phone from the zipper compartment on the side. The screen displayed a phone number she didn't recognize. It was clearly not a Portland number.

Although she wouldn't normally, her instincts told her to answer the call. "Hello," she said, and there was a long pause. So much so Liza pulled the phone from her ear for a second to check and see if the caller had hung up. "Hello," a sexy voice finally said. "Is Tate available?"

"No, she is not," Liza all but growled. The last thing she expected was to hear a sensual woman's voice coming through Tate's phone and asking for her. "Who is this?"

Liza would swear she could hear the woman smiling, and not in a nice way. "I am Tate's new coworker," she said. "I have a few more questions about some of her top clients."

"I'm sure this can wait until tomorrow," Liza snapped. "Like I said, she's not available."

That time, the caller really did chuckle. "What a shame," she said. "I'll just have to catch her at work in the morning." Before Liza could come back with a reply the line went dead.

Coming out of the bathroom wrapped in her robe with her hair still wet, Tate froze when she saw Liza pulling things haphazardly out of her dresser drawers. "What are you doing?" she asked but already knew the answer. It was the last thing she wanted to have happen.

Hearing her question, the woman whirled around, and Tate saw she had been crying. "I'm going to a hotel," Liza said. "I don't want to be here anymore."

Tate shook her head. "I don't understand. What happened?"

"I'm sorry, but I answered your phone."

At Liza's words, Tate felt a sinking feeling in her stomach. "Why?"

Tilting her head, Liza regarded Tate with a look she couldn't quite read. "Interesting response," Liza said, narrowing her eyes. "And you didn't ask who it was." Sucking in a breath Tate realized her mistake but her instinct had told her only one person would be calling late tonight. The woman who seemed intent on making her life hell for some reason.

Plus, Tate calculated only one person would make Liza so upset. "You're right," Tate replied. "I made an assumption based on how you're acting. Was it Aurora Price?"

"She didn't give her name, but she did say she was a new coworker," Liza said turning back to the dresser and pulling out more clothing. "Someone who sounded sexy and said she was looking forward to 'catching you in the morning'. As you'd expect, I didn't appreciate that little comment." Swallowing hard, Tate took a step forward and reached for Liza's elbow. Liza jerked away. "Don't touch me. Just let me do this."

"No," Tate said. "If anyone is leaving it will be me."

Liza stopped. "And where exactly would you go? Back to work?"

"Stop thinking that way," Tate said firmly. "I would go to Nikki's and sleep on her couch. You know that."

Slowly Liza turned to face Tate, her eyes glimmering with tears. "I don't know anything at this point," she said. "I feel like my world has been turned upside down."

Moving in closer, Tate risked putting her hand gently on Liza's arm. "You know I love you," she said. "I have loved you since the minute I saw you, and nothing is going to stop that."

"But, Tate," Liza said, but didn't pull away. Tate moved

closer until she could put her arms around the woman's waist. "What is happening?"

"Nothing we can't work our way through," Tate said. "I promise. Come to bed and let me show you how much I love you."

## 11

The white dress was stunning. Everything about it was exactly like she imagined since she was a little girl. Intricate pearl beading danced across the layers of white silk wrapped around her body. A two-tier cut matching bridal veil cascaded down the back of her head and shoulders. "You look so beautiful," Allie said from beside her, and when Liza looked at their reflection in the mirror, her friend had tears in her eyes.

"I'm so happy for you," Rey added from the other side, and the two women stepped in to give Liza a group hug. Feeling the love of her friends and the specialness of the moment, Liza's heart swelled with emotion. Finally, the waiting was over, and her wedding day had arrived. So far it was everything she wished for. Her best friends were with her, and as she gazed in the mirror, she realized she looked gorgeous. *A beautiful bride at last*, she thought and then waved her hand at her face to fight back tears of her own. She didn't want to mess up her perfect makeup.

Giving Liza a kiss on her cheek, Allie backed away. "We'll see you in there," Allie said. "From the front row."

Before they went, Liza turned, grabbing the hands of her two best friends. "Thank you for being here with me on my special day."

"There is no place in the world we would rather be," Rey said. "It's a magical day." Then they were gone, and Liza was left alone for a moment. Everything seemed so surreal, that she was standing there in her wedding dress about to walk down the aisle to finally be joined in matrimony with Tate. Somehow, she didn't know quite how she got there or even remember picking out the dress. Furrowing her brow, she tried to recall those events, but before she could, there was a tap at the dressing room door.

Opening it, she saw her father standing there in a tuxedo. "It's time," he said. "I've waited to escort you down the aisle for way too long." Tears threatened again as Liza took in his words. She loved how much her family embraced Tate and knew she was lucky to have them at her side while she married the woman she loved.

In an instant, she was waiting at a doorway, ready to walk down the aisle. Her arm was looped through her father's, and she was ready for the music to start. But when it didn't, she grew confused. The waiting seemed to go on forever and finally she stepped forward to look into the room where everyone sat watching. She blinked with surprise. The wedding had already started without her. *What is happening?* she wondered. *How could this go on without me?* Then she saw Tate was at the altar and holding the hands of a different bride. Someone who was not Liza. Reality crashed in on her as she realized Tate was marrying someone else. *She isn't against getting married*, Liza thought. *She is only against getting married to me.*

Suddenly, all she wanted to do was flee. She turned but the elaborate dress wrapped around her legs. Unable to move, she felt like she was falling and as she reached out to brace herself, she jolted awake. For a second she didn't know where she was and then realized she was in the bed she shared with Tate every night. The sheets were wrapped around her, and she fought them off trying to breathe. It had been a dream. *Actually, I would call that a nightmare*, Liza thought as she sat up. Rubbing her face with her hands, she tried to shake the horrible feelings from the dream. *Are they a sign of something I've been ignoring?* She paused, then shook her head. *No. Tate loves me and no one else. I can feel it in my heart.*

Looking around the room she noticed a note sitting on the nightstand. Picking up the piece of paper, she read the words written in Tate's handwriting. "Please be patient while I work this out. I need your love but also your trust." Liza sighed. She did love Tate but after the strange phone call from the night before, followed by her nightmare, she didn't know what to think. More than anything though, she would rather have had a conversation that morning over coffee rather than be left a simple note. If only Tate had made a little more time for her.

TATE WAS ON A MISSION. For the second day in a row, she skipped her morning workout and was at the office early. Today her agenda had only one thing at the top of the list—to corner Chad and find out what the hell was going on. She needed to know all the facts regarding the situation with Aurora Price, and it couldn't wait any longer. Unfortunately, when she got to her desk and checked the computer to see the man's schedule, he was double and triple booked throughout the day. There wasn't even time at lunch available. "Shit," Tate muttered under her breath as she leaned back in her office chair and contemplated her options. She could stake out his office door and hope to catch him in between meetings but that would look particularly desperate. Plus, she knew his executive assistant would likely shoo her away.

*So, what are my options?* she thought, pinching the bridge of her nose. *There has to be some way I can reach him.* Trying to catch him after work would mean another late night in the office, which would not go over well with Liza. The last two nights had been rough, and she didn't want to repeat it a third time in a row. *No, staying late is not an option.* Then an idea came to her. Glancing at her watch she realized her boss would be arriving at the building any second. Her best chance for an opening was to cross paths with him in the lobby.

Jumping up from her desk she rushed to the elevators. Waiting impatiently until the doors finally opened, she let people out before quickly stepping inside and pushing L for the lobby. The ride seemed to take forever, but after less than a minute, the elevator arrived in the broad lobby. People were walking in through the revolving door that led outside. Even though it was early, quite a few people were arriving, because the financial world never slept. Being on the west coast put them a little behind accounts on the east coast, and so it wasn't unusual for the office to be filled well before eight in the morning. Trying to look inconspicuous as people she knew passed her, Tate waited until she saw Chad's gray-haired head above the crowd as he came into the lobby. Dressed in an expensive navy-blue suit and carrying a laptop bag, he crossed toward the elevators. Seeing her opening, Tate made her move and fell into step beside him. "Good morning, Chad," she said making the man look at her with surprise.

"Well good morning, Tate," he said after a moment, but his narrowed eyes making it clear he was a little suspicious of her sudden appearance. "What are you doing in the lobby?"

"Just checking on some things," Tate lied as she watched him push the button to call the elevators. "But I'm glad I caught up with you. We need to talk about this new situation with Aurora Price." Other people had started to gather to wait for the elevator, and Chad's face showed displeasure.

It was as if he did not want to talk about things in front of a crowd. "We can talk about that in my office," he said as the doors opened, and they stepped aboard.

"I'm fine with that," Tate said. "I hope it will be a short conversation."

FINALLY DRAGGING herself out of bed, Liza stumbled her way to the kitchen to make a cup of coffee. After her horrible dream, she had shut off the alarm on her phone and sent a text to her boss that she wasn't feeling well and would be late. Even though she tried to go back to sleep, whenever she closed her eyes, she saw Tate at the altar with someone else. For some reason she could not shake the feeling it was some kind of omen.

As the coffee percolated, she took a can of wet cat food from the fridge and set it on the counter. Usually that sound alone was enough to bring their cat Zombie running into the kitchen, but surprisingly, he did not arrive. Even after she picked his plate off the floor and put a serving on it, there was still no sign of her little buddy. "That's weird," she said to the empty kitchen. "It's not like he ever missed a meal." Thankfully, Zombie was an entirely indoor cat, so she wasn't worried he had gotten lost in the neighborhood overnight, but there was a possibility he had found his way into the garage when Tate left that morning.

Hurrying to check, she was about ready to open the back

door when she heard a pitiful meow. Turning to look down the hall, she saw the door to Tate's office was closed. *Why would Tate have closed that?* she wondered as she walked to open it. Zombie streamed out as if he had been abandoned for centuries and was starving to death. Stepping out of his way, Liza was about to follow him back to the kitchen when she had the strongest desire to look around Tate's office. It was so unusual for the woman to have closed the door that morning. *What has she been doing in here?* The last time she was inside, Tate was drowning her sorrows with bourbon.

Flipping on the light, Liza walked to the desk and let her eyes scan the surface but saw nothing unusual. There was a five by seven picture of her and Tate, arms around each other and with sunburnt noses, on a sandy beach in Hawaii. The shot was of their first vacation away together and the time in paradise had been nothing short of magical. They seemed so far away from those giddy days and nights in the tropical sun that she felt a pang of sadness. Life had moved on so much and yet in some ways it hadn't at all. Although they had been together for years and experienced many more vacations, they still weren't married to each other.

Circling the desk, she casually opened the middle drawer and looked to see nothing but an assortment of pens, notepads, paperclips, and the like. Totally ordinary so she closed the drawer planning to leave, but then hesitated. A part of her was still curious. Reaching to open the top drawer of the desk, she was surprised to find it locked. Giving another tug, she stood straighter and stared at the handle as if it had offended her. *Why is this locked?* she wondered. *What does Tate have in there?* Although Liza didn't spend much time in Tate's office, she was certain the woman never locked any of the drawers before. Suddenly, she had the strongest desire to search for the key and see what was in the drawer but then guilt washed over her. These were Tate's things in her personal space. Although they shared everything, they also had to respect each other's privacy. There was no doubt a very good reason why the desk drawer was locked. Leaving the office, Liza stood in the doorway and looked around one last time before closing the door. *Definitely Tate's space. Not mine.* For the first time Liza wondered what else Tate might keep secret in her life.

12

Tate rode the elevator with Chad in complete silence. No one in the car said a word, each fixated on their phone. Her boss didn't make any comment until he whisked them past the executive assistant's desk and into his office where he shut the door. "I feel like you ambushed me in the lobby," he said as he took off his jacket and hung it on the coat rack beside the door. "And let me guess—this is about Aurora Price."

"I won't lie," Tate said. "That's exactly what I was doing. Your schedule is full today and you were unavailable all day yesterday but this needs to be discussed."

"Fine," Chad said getting into the chair behind his desk. He leaned back. "Please have a seat and tell me what there is to discuss."

Taking one of the two chairs in front of Chad's desk, Tate was a little taken aback by the fact her boss didn't seem to think there was anything to discuss. *How could he not understand I would be upset about not getting the promotion?* she wondered. *Or is it really just all my head?* Suddenly feeling a little less confident, Tate swallowed hard. "Well, I guess I'm simply not sure I understand the relationship between Aurora Price and me."

Chad nodded. "You're right. We should make that clearer." He reached for his desk phone. "Hold on. Let's see if she's in."

Tate opened her mouth to tell him the last thing she wanted was to have a three-person meeting on the topic. Unfortunately, she was too late to complain as he picked up the receiver and punched in a number. After a beat, he smiled. "Good morning. Aurora, can you meet me in my office?" After a beat where Tate guessed Aurora agreed, Chad nodded, hanging up before leaning back in his chair again and steepling his fingers. "She should be right here. But I want you to know how much I appreciate that you're such a team player. You're a valuable asset to this firm."

"Thank you," Tate mumbled, unable to find the courage to tell him what she really thought.

They sat there in an awkward silence for minute until there was a sharp knock at Chad's office door. "Come in," Chad called, and the door opened to show Aurora Price. She was dressed as attractively as the last two days. A dark green pencil skirt with a flowing cream blouse all accenting her auburn hair.

Her eyes landed on Tate and, for a second, there was a flicker of surprise, but then she smiled. "I hadn't expected to see you here this morning," she said walking in with a toss of her head. "A nice surprise."

"Actually, Tate's who I want to talk about," Chad said. "I want to make sure you both understand your relationship."

For a second Aurora slowed her steps, and Tate was sure she saw a hint of concern in the woman's eyes before she recovered. With nothing but confident grace, she sat in one of the chairs in front of Chad's desk. "I'm all ears," she said, and Chad smiled as he tapped the desktop with a pen.

"Good," Chad said. "Let's keep this simple." He pointed the pen at Tate. "I want you to start reporting to Aurora."

"But—" Tate tried to interrupt, but Chad shook his head.

"I've made up my mind," he continued. "Until she's up to speed, I basically want you attached at the hip. Does that make sense?"

Tate felt her stomach clench. It was the last thing she wanted to hear but didn't know how else to respond. "Yes, sir," she said and couldn't miss the smug smile on Aurora Price's face.

LOOKING at the clock on the wall, Liza could hardly believe it was only two in the afternoon. The day crawled, and all she wanted was for it to be over so she could go home and open a bottle of wine. She was ready to try and console herself on the couch after hours of being unable to shake the feeling she didn't know Tate as well as she thought. The phone call from some woman the night before mixed with finding a locked drawer worried her. The ridiculous possibility Tate might have a whole different life kept circling in her mind. It was insane and probably influenced by some of the drama television shows she watched, but it still nagged at her. In her heart, she knew Tate was the most trustworthy and honest person she had ever met, but for some reason that couldn't stop her racing mind.

Between phone calls, Liza checked her cell and noticed she had a text from Allie. "Would you mind if we don't have game night tonight?" Liza raised an eyebrow. *Is it only Wednesday?* she wondered. The last few days had seemed a blur but felt like they had taken weeks. Yet a glance at her desk calendar confirmed it was indeed Wednesday. It was a long-standing tradition that every week her group of friends gathered at one of their homes to play board games or cards.

The meetup was a way for them to break up the week and have some fun. *I bet Tate has forgotten too. We've both had our minds occupied.* Considering how things were between her and Tate, she certainly didn't care if they canceled.

She typed it into her phone. "That's fine with me."

"Okay," Allie wrote back after a beat. "But I still want you to help me tonight."

Liza frowned. "Help with what?"

"Come to Ruby's after work and brainstorm with the gang," Allie wrote. With a sigh, Liza tried to think of an excuse to send to Allie. She was not in the mood to be with her friends and brainstorm. All she wanted was a bottle of wine and a pity party of her own.

On the flipside, she didn't want to let them down. "What are we brainstorming?"

"We need to figure out what to do at Pride! It's this weekend!"

*Is it already here?* Liza thought and sighed. She couldn't say no. *Maybe getting away from the house will be good for me tonight*, she thought. Certainly, the last two evenings at home had been a hell. "All right, I'll be there," she wrote, and Allie messaged right back.

"Wonderful. Do you think Tate will be able to come too?" *That's the million-dollar question*, Liza thought. It seemed highly unlikely that Tate would be rushing home tonight let alone be willing to socialize.

Still, she wanted to give the woman the benefit of the doubt. "I'll text her," Liza wrote and then the phone on her desk rang. "Gotta go."

Luckily the customer was pleasant, and the call went smoothly. After she hung up, she decided to go ahead and text Tate. Figuring it was a futile attempt, but having promised Allie, Liza typed a message. "Can you come to Ruby's tonight? Everyone will be there to talk about Pride."

There was a long pause, and Liza shook her head. Silence yet again. She was about to put her phone away when it vibrated. A text from Tate.

Looking at the screen Liza was surprised to see a short but promising message. "I'll be there. Ruby's sounds great." After a second, there was another text. A heart emoji. Liza felt her body relax a little as warmth filled her chest. *Maybe things will be all right after all.*

Already running late, Tate hurried into her office to shut down her laptop and head for Ruby's. It was five-thirty, and she had hoped to be out of there thirty minutes before. She wanted to make sure Liza and their friends felt like they were a priority in her life. It was time to put some normalcy back into things. Packed and slipping on her lightweight jacket, Tate slipped the bag's strap over her shoulder and headed for her door. Suddenly, Aurora appeared in the doorway, making Tate pull up short. "Oh, you're leaving?" Aurora said as she put a hand on the doorframe as if planning to physically bar Tate from leaving. "I was hoping I could catch you for a few more minutes."

Not wanting to be rude to the woman Chad had made her temporary boss, Tate held back her frustration and paused. "What can I help with?" she asked, and Aurora smiled.

As always, it was charismatic but also a little calculated. "I have an idea," she said. "One that I think can save the firm a lot of money, and I want to run it by you."

Unable to help but be curious by such a bold statement, Tate raised her eyebrows. "All right I'm listening," she said, and Aurora shook her head.

"Not standing here in the doorway," she said. "Follow me to my office and we can discuss it in private."

Tate wasn't so sure if she was interested in hearing whatever Aurora had to say. Somehow her offer felt like a ploy, although she didn't quite understand why the woman would want to play games with her. Yet over the last three days, that sensation had slowly started to build. It was especially odd because Tate was certain she made it clear that she had a girlfriend. *Not to mention we are in a workspace*, she thought, and started to decline.

As if reading her mind Aurora took a step closer. For a second it seemed like she was going to reach out and touch Tate's sleeve but then her hand stopped midair. "Tate, I think what I am planning will help your career," she said softly, meeting Tate's eye. "Both our careers." Not sure exactly what she meant, Tate frowned. *Does she think I need her help with my career?* she wondered. *Does this have something to do with my missed promotion?*

It was all so confusing, and Tate realized then and there she did not want anything to do with it tonight. "It can wait until tomorrow," she said and motioned toward the door to usher them out.

"Really?" Aurora said with a hint of disbelief, but also something else. She seemed irritated. "And here I thought you were dedicated to your job."

Tate stiffened at the dig. The last thing she wanted was for anyone to accuse her of anything but complete dedication. "Fine," she said through clenched teeth. "I'll give you ten minutes."

"Perfect," Aurora said, walking down the hallway without even looking back to make sure Tate followed. As they reached her office, Aurora hesitated at the door. "You know…" She looked at Tate. "I have a better idea. Let's discuss this over dinner."

"I'm not sure that's going to work for me," Tate immediately said, and Aurora lifted her chin.

"And why is that?"

"Because I have plans for the evening," Tate replied. "That I'm already late for."

"Plans that are more important than this firm and your career with it?" Aurora asked, her voice filled with mock surprise. "Chad will be so disappointed." The veiled threat filled the space between them.

Closing her eyes, Tate took a deep breath and then let it out slowly before looking at the woman again. *Liza is going to kill me for being so late,* she thought. *But what can I do?* "A quick dinner," she said. "I have a place in mind."

Aurora's face lit up. "That's fine," she said. "I'll follow you wherever you want to go."

13

Walking through the door at Ruby's, Liza hadn't realized how much she missed the place. Not that it had been particularly long since she visited, but she had missed the warm atmosphere in the presence of her friends. Walking in the direction of their usual booth, Liza saw Allie look over before her friend gave her a big smile.

"You made it," Allie said, standing from the booth and enveloping Liza into a big hug.

"It's good to be here," Liza said meaning every word, pulling back to see Vivian and Marty there as well. "Marty, I haven't seen you in forever."

Marty smiled a little sheepishly. "I have been working double shifts now that the head baker has decided to retire and is showing me all the ropes."

"Plus spending extra time with Rey," Allie added in a playful tone.

"Well that too," Marty said as her grin widened. "We're still trying to get to know each other on a deeper level."

Vivian chuckled, the sound deep and warm. "Getting to know each other?" she said. "Is that what they call it now?"

Marty blushed to the roots of her blonde hair and Liza laughed. It felt good. The last few days had been a torture and she needed exactly this kind of break.

Vivian slid from the booth. "What can I make you?" Vivian asked as Marty stood to let Liza slide in.

"I'll take a margarita on the rocks."

"Coming right up," Vivian said. "Salt or no salt today?"

Liza tilted her head and thought about the question because she went back and forth depending on her mood and decided that today she felt salty. "Salt," she answered. "Make it heavy. And don't hold back on the tequila either."

Vivian nodded. "You got it," she said while Liza relaxed on the booth's vinyl seat.

Reaching across the table, Allie took Liza's hand and gave it a squeeze. "I'm so glad you're here," she said. "How are things?" Before Liza could figure out how best to answer, the door to Ruby's opened again and Rey, followed by Nikki, walked in. Marty got up and met Rey halfway, giving her a quick kiss. The depth of their tenderness toward each other gave Liza a little pang of jealousy. She remembered what those early days with Tate had been like, full of little kisses and heated looks. All of that seemed far away, and she could only hope they would get it back.

Slipping past them, Nikki grinned. "Okay, lovebirds," she said as she joined Liza on the bench. "Hey. Is Tate going to be here?"

Liza nodded. "Her text said she would," she said, with a glance at her watch. It was already almost six, and she had hoped Tate would be at Ruby's by now. A hint of anxiety fluttered in Liza's stomach. *Or will she choose to work late again?* she wondered. *With that woman from the phone call?*

"Well, I hope so," Nikki said. "She skipped our workout again this morning."

Liza raised her eyebrows. It was rare for Tate to miss a

workout. She thought that was why she left so early. "I guess she had to go to the office early," Liza explained trying to cover her initial reaction and was thankful when Rey and Marty approached the booth to join them.

"Hi," Rey said. "Sorry I'm late. The streetcar was running behind schedule."

"I see," Nikki murmured, still focused on Liza while giving her a suspicious look.

"We're just glad you made it," Allie said before turning to the group. "So, about Pride." Liza appreciated her friend changing the subject and gave her a small smile. "We need to figure out what's going on with Ruby's booth. We were able to grab a great location at the last minute because someone else cancelled, and we want to make it interesting. Really draw people to it."

Vivian returned to the table and set down a tray of margaritas. "But with something original," she added.

"I'm sure we can come up with something," Nikki said.

"Exactly," Marty added as she and Rey sat with them. "This is the most creative group I know."

Slipping from the booth to stand, Nikki nodded. "But maybe we should get dinner first," she said. "I'm starving, and I think I heard we were having Greek."

"If that's all right," Allie asked.

"Absolutely," everyone seemed to say at once.

"Perfect. I'll go to Uncle Peter's cart and grab us all something," Nikki said. "Liza, will you walk with me and help carry everything back?"

Liza was a little surprised at the request. Normally Nikki would've taken Marty but then she realized Nikki wanted to be alone with her. *No doubt to give me the third degree*, she thought. *I can't blame her.* "I can do that," Liza said. Slipping from the booth, she looked at the group. "We will be right back.

. . .

As Aurora Price followed Tate through the Pearl District of Portland in her Audi TT, Tate wondered what the hell she was doing. *Why did I cave into her?* she wondered. *I need to get to Ruby's and back to Liza.* Yet she did know why—her career. If what Aurora said was true and she could be part of saving the firm lots of money, it might be what she needed to get over the last hurdle toward a promotion she knew she deserved. *I'll make sure we keep it short.* At least she had been smart enough to think of a restaurant near Ruby's. That would save a lot of time later. There was a little Italian place two blocks away where she knew the service was good but also quick.

Pulling into a parking garage across the street from the restaurant, she slowed to make sure Aurora saw where she turned. The little red car was right on her bumper, and Tate led the way to a pair of spaces one level up. Getting out, Aurora was all smiles as she looked over the top of her low-profile car. "This is so exciting," she said. "I've been trying to find new places in Portland to explore. Even with our short drive through this neighborhood, I can see there are many little shops and restaurants I need to try."

Tate nodded. "Yes, the Pearl District is known for that sort of thing." As she started walking toward the elevators, Aurora fell into step beside her, and their shoulders bumped. The woman was walking so close to her, Tate felt uncomfortable and veered a little to the left to add space.

Yet when they reached the elevator and she pushed the button to go down, Aurora closed in again, only this time put her hand on Tate's arm. "I don't suppose this area also has a gym? Maybe somewhere you like to go," she said, her eyes taking on a sultry look. "I mean clearly..." She ran a finger down Tate's sleeve. "...you work out."

Tate felt her face flush from the touch, but not from attraction. The sensual gesture embarrassed her. For whatever reason, Aurora was attracted to her, and there was no mistaking it.

Again, she stepped back and that time a hint of displeasure showed on Aurora's face. "I do go to a gym near here," Tate said, not sure she wanted to give more information than that. The gym was special to her and having Aurora show up would ruin things. Luckily the elevator arrived, and when they stepped inside, Tate made sure she stood near the wall away from Aurora.

Neither said anything on the ride down, but once they were on the sidewalk and walking in the direction of the restaurant, Aurora started again. "So, this place we are going to, is it special to you?"

"Not really," Tate answered. "It's relatively new, and I've only been there once." She looked at Aurora. "With my girlfriend."

"Yes," Aurora said. "Your girlfriend. Who I spoke with on your phone." Her smile was smug. "I'm not sure she appreciated my call."

Tate didn't see any reason to answer as they reached the restaurant. Out of habit, she held the door for Aurora to step through. As soon as she did it, Tate wanted to kick herself. Aurora's glance over her shoulder told Tate it had been a mistake. Clearly the woman was reading any kind gesture as flirtation. With a sigh, Tate stepped up to the hostess. "Table for two," she said.

"Right this way," the woman said and led them through the restaurant to a nice place near the corner windows.

As Tate sat, her phone buzzed, and she had no doubt it was Liza wondering where the hell she was. "I need to look at this," Tate said as she fished her phone out of her pocket.

"Of course," Aurora said, meeting her eye. "This is after

work hours." There was a hint of suggestiveness in her tone that Tate didn't like, but she let it go to read the text.

"We are at Uncle Peter's getting dinner," Liza's text said. "Do you want a gyro or a souvlaki wrap?"

"Souvlaki," Tate sent back. "I'll be there soon."

With multiple bags of Greek food in hand, Liza and Nikki started back to Ruby's. "Thank you for coming with me," Nikki said, and Liza glanced at her.

"I thought you were going to give me the third degree, she said. "About how Tate and I are doing."

Nikki shrugged. "I thought about it," she said. "But then changed my mind."

"Why is that?" Liza asked. "I know you're concerned."

Nodding, Nikki adjusted the bags in her hands. "I am concerned a little," she said. "But I know how much you and Tate love each other, so I am giving you the benefit of the doubt." She gave Liza her charismatic smile. "It will be good to have you both at Ruby's tonight."

"Yes," Liza said. "Ruby's is special, and it is where we met, so—" Out of the corner of her eye, Liza saw something that made her heart nearly stop. She froze on the sidewalk and stared.

Nikki took a couple more steps but then paused as well and followed Liza's gaze. "Oh shit," Nikki muttered under her breath, but Liza was already in motion. Through the window she clearly saw Tate sitting at a dinner table with another woman. Someone with long auburn hair.

Storming inside she brushed by the hostess and made a beeline for the table where her girlfriend sat with someone else. At the last second, Tate glanced over, and her eyes widened when she saw Liza. *She looks guilty*, Liza thought for a fleeting moment. *Maybe this is what she's been doing behind my back all long.*

"What the hell?" Liza spat, making the woman with Tate turn to look. Liza sucked in a breath when she saw the woman's face. She was gorgeous. One of those people who could easily be mistaken for a beautiful celebrity. Big green eyes, beautiful hair flowing to her shoulders, sensual lips, and light skin—qualities the dark-haired Liza didn't have but maybe Tate wanted. *Well, clearly she does*, Liza thought. *Or she wouldn't be here with her instead of at Ruby's with me.*

Tate stood. "Liza," she started. "This is not what you think." Before she said another word, the stranger with her stood as well and extended a hand. Liza, who still held two bags of food, simply stared at the woman's gesture.

After a moment of hesitation, the auburn-haired woman dropped her hand, but a big smile still lit up her beautiful face. "You must be…" the woman looked at Tate. "I'm sorry I don't know your girlfriend's name." Liza looked at Tate and her embarrassment was clear. "Or at least I am assuming this is your girlfriend."

"Yes," Tate said. "This is my girlfriend."

"Are you so sure?" Liza asked. "You seem confused."

"Liza," Tate started again and reached for her.

Liza pulled back. "Don't touch me," she said. "This must be the infamous Aurora Price. Am I wrong?"

"You're not wrong," Aurora said. "I'm Tate's new coworker."

Shaking her head, Liza lifted her chin. "Right," she said. "Sure. Well, I've seen enough." The threat of tears made her want to retreat. The last thing she would do was cry in front of Tate or that woman.

Suddenly Nikki was beside her. "Liza," she said. "We should go."

There was a coolness in her tone that let Liza know her

friend was disappointed with Tate as well. "Yes, let's get back to our real friends," Liza said, turning on her heel to storm out of the restaurant.

"Liza, wait," Tate said and as Liza left the building, she realized not only Nikki, but Tate followed her. "Listen to me."

When they reached the sidewalk, Liza whirled on her girlfriend. "What more is there to say?" Liza asked and Tate shook her head.

"I am serious," she said. "It is not what you're thinking."

"Sure, my eyes were tricking me," Liza said, reaching into one of the bags to pull out a container of food. "Here's your dinner." The tears from before disappeared replaced with fury. "I got you your souvlaki." Then she opened the container and, with all her might, threw it at Tate where it splatted against the woman's chest. "But apparently you aren't going to need it."

14

As the Greek food container dropped from her chest leaving a mess of tzatziki sauce and feta cheese, Tate's temper flared. She had had enough. In her mind, Liza's attack was unwarranted and throwing food at her in front of the restaurant where anyone could be watching was not acceptable. Her girlfriend was jumping to conclusions, and Tate needed to make her understand, but yelling on the street in Portland was not how to get it done. Yelling was not her style under any circumstance for that matter. *And I'm not going to start now,* she thought. *I need to stay calm and handle Liza gently. She's hurting, that's all this is.* Taking a deep breath to center herself, Tate looked Liza in the eye. "Please calm down. It is a work dinner. Nothing more," she said, but before she could continue Aurora Price stepped up beside her.

"Tate," she said. "How can I help?"

"Oh, I think you've helped enough," Liza growled, taking two steps toward Aurora. Luckily, Nikki responded quickly and took Liza by the arm before the messy confrontation escalated.

Impressively, Aurora didn't flinch. "I think you should do as Tate advises and calm down," she said. "You're overreacting. We were discussing work."

For a moment Liza's eyes seemed confused, and Tate felt a sliver of hope things would get straightened out, but then the anger snapped back into them again. "This seems like too much of a coincidence to me," she said. "And I don't want to interrupt your 'work dinner.'" With that she shrugged Nikki off and turned to walk away. Starting to follow Liza, Nikki glanced back and met Tate's eyes. There was a hint of sympathy, but also a hint of honest doubt. Tate hated seeing that almost more than hurting Liza. She couldn't stand it if Nikki suspected her too.

Wanting to follow them back to Ruby's, Tate headed toward the restaurant to get her bag, but Aurora was still beside her. "I'm sorry," she said, and Tate could not help but stare at her.

"Are you really?" she asked in a quiet voice. "I told you I had plans tonight and yet you insisted."

A hint of color rose to Aurora's cheeks. "I assumed you were adult enough to make the best decision," she said. "And this was important. Perhaps more important than a girlfriend who flies off the handle before there's an explanation."

Tate narrowed her eyes ready to tell Aurora she should not say anything about Liza, but then she shook her head, and walked into the restaurant to get her things. She would go to Ruby's and try to convince Liza to listen. All her friends would be there, and it would take a lot of nerve to walk up to the table if Liza had told them her suspicions. *I can handle it*, she thought. *And I know they won't judge me without more proof, and there isn't any more proof to be found.* There was nothing but a misunderstanding, and Tate would make sure they all knew it.

. . .

SLAMMING through the door at Ruby's, Liza had never been more hurt and confused than at that moment. Seeing Tate through the restaurant window, having dinner with another woman, and an absolutely gorgeous woman at that, brought back every bit of her fears from her dream. *It was as if I somehow had a premonition*, Liza thought. *That maybe Tate has found someone else.* Yet she wasn't a hundred percent sure of what to think. Tate and the other woman had both insisted it was nothing but work. What didn't make sense was if Tate was going to have a work meeting why did she not tell Liza. *She lied to me.*

With Nikki still behind her, Liza walked across Ruby's to where her friends sat. When they glanced over, Liza saw concern light up their faces. Marty stood and met her a few steps from the booth, taking the bag of food from her hand. "What happened?" she asked, looking from Liza, then to Nikki, and back.

Liza shook her head angrily. "I'm not even sure where to begin," she said. "It was just horrible. Nikki can explain."

Nikki sighed. "Liza is right, it is bordering on horrible. We found Tate," she said. "Having dinner with a coworker."

Liza saw Rey and Allie look at each other before Rey raised her eyebrows. "Is this the coworker who took Tate's promotion?" she asked. "Aurora something?"

"Aurora Price," Liza said. "Who Tate failed to mention is a gorgeous woman. I mean, movie star gorgeous."

For a beat, no one said a word as they absorbed the information. "I'm sure it's a misunderstanding," Rey finally said. "Surely they were there for a reason other than what you're thinking."

Liza felt tears burn her eyes as she tried to give Tate the benefit of the doubt, but the image of her standing at the altar with someone else stuck with her. "I'm not sure," Liza said. "I just don't know what to think."

The door to Ruby's opened again, and when they all looked, it was Tate. The expression on her face was one of both concern and frustration. Thankfully, Aurora was not with her. *That would've been too much*, Liza thought. *I never want to see her in here.*

"Liza," Tate said in an exasperated tone. "We need to talk."

"I have nothing to say to you," Liza said. "Maybe later but not right now."

"Then when?"

Liza shook her head. "I don't know the answer to that. But I don't want to rake our friends through this."

Even though the people in the booth, who she dearly loved more than family, would never judge them, the situation between her and Tate needed to be handled in private.

"Then just come home, and let's find a way to work through this," Tate said.

Liza shook her head. "No," she said. "I'm not coming home with you right now. I'm going to a hotel."

"I don't want that," Tate said, and Liza watched her face fall. "I'll sleep on the couch or whatever you want, but I need you to come home."

Liza felt a tug of sympathy to see Tate look so sad, but it wasn't enough to convince her to stay there for at least one night. "Not tonight," she said.

"Then tonight you will stay with us," Allie said from behind her. "We have a guest room all made up, and you are welcome to it."

Relief washed over Liza at her friend's offer. "Are you sure?" she asked, knowing Allie would insist but wanting to be fair. "I don't want to inconvenience you or Vivian."

"I'm sure," Allie replied. "Come over and take a time out."

. . .

Feeling some relief knowing Liza would be staying with Allie and Vivian instead of alone in a hotel, Tate nodded. "Thank you," she said meeting Allie's eye before looking at Liza again. "I'll call you later tonight and check on you."

"You don't need to check on me," Liza said, crossing her arms. "I can take care of myself."

Starting to feel a hint of anger returning at the woman stubbornness, Tate forced herself not to react. "I'll call just the same, and if you don't want to answer that's fine," she said. "And if you will all excuse me, I'm not in an emotional place to be of much use tonight, so I'm going to go."

"Of course," Allie said, and Vivian nodded.

"I think it's best if we all brainstorm later on this," Vivian said, while Nikki put the bags of food she'd been holding on the table before turning to Tate.

"Let me walk you to your car," she said.

Tate let out a deep breath and nodded. "I appreciate that," she said and with a nod to the group, she left with her friend to go back to the restaurant where Tate's car was still parked in the lot across the street. As they walked, both were quiet for the first block, but when they waited at the light to cross the street, Tate had to know what Nikki was thinking. "Do you believe me? That what you saw tonight was work and only work?"

When they started moving again, Nikki did not reply, and Tate started to think the worst. She opened her mouth to say more, but Nikki held up a hand. "I believe you," she said. "But it does look bad. What is going on with you right now? Not only did you bail on our friends tonight, but you've skipped a couple of workouts. You never do that."

"I'm not even sure where to start," Tate said as they took the elevator and stopped by her car. "It's all somehow mixed up in my not getting the promotion." She shook her head. "I do know this woman Aurora Price swooped in and spoiled everything. Not only professionally, but now maybe my relationship with Liza." Pausing, Tate wasn't sure if she should keep talking, but then Nikki was her best friend and it felt right. "Can I tell you something and have you not repeat it to anyone?"

Nikki did not hesitate. "Of course," she said. "You can always trust me."

Tate gave her a small smile. "I know," she said, already feeling some relief of being able to share her thoughts. She took a deep breath to gather herself. "I know this sounds crazy, but I think Aurora Price is sexually harassing me at work. Or at least is on the verge."

Nikki let out a whistle as she rocked back on her heels. "Oh, that is not good."

"Definitely not. And she's doing it even though I told her I had a girlfriend from the start."

Her face turning serious, Nikki met Tate's eye. "What is she doing to you?"

"She makes subtle comments on the borderline of inappropriate," she said. "Sometimes stands too close to me, even ran a finger down my sleeve tonight."

"I see," Nikki said as she looked thoughtfully into the distance. "That makes this even more complicated."

"Yeah, it does," Tate said. "I'm afraid if I go to anyone at work to complain they'll think it's sour grapes and not believe me. Besides, I can't prove anything. It's my word over hers when she is basically my boss right now."

Nikki frowned. "I don't know what to say, but we need to fix this."

"I know," Tate replied. "And quickly."

## 15

It was not until she had buckled her seatbelt in the car that Liza let herself cry. As Allie pulled out of the small parking lot behind Ruby's, Liza covered her face with her hands and sobbed. She was thankful Allie was wise enough to simply drive and let the tears come, not saying a word until Liza had a moment to get it out before finding her composure. Rubbing her eyes to clear them, Liza sucked in a shaky breath. "Thank you so much, Allie," she said. "I appreciate your offer, but I really can go to a hotel. I don't want you to feel like you were put on the spot."

"Absolutely not," Allie said, reaching to touch Liza's thigh and give it a pat. "We have plenty of space, and I want you to feel welcome for as long as you need."

"You're a good friend," Liza said, before a half sob escaped. She shook her head. "I just don't know what's happening between me and Tate."

Putting on her turn signal and coming to a stop at the light, Allie nodded slowly as she looked out the windshield. "Things do seem a little unclear between you," she said. "And I'm sure that sounds like an understatement."

"A little," Liza said with a tearful laugh. "I can't believe it's only been three days since you and Rey and I were at the shopping mall mooning over the engagement rings." She swallowed hard. "Life has taken such a scary turn."

"I'm sure," Allie said, speeding up again as they headed down Glisan Street toward the waterfront. "But…"

When she hesitated, Liza looked at her. "But what?"

Allie bit her lip before answering then said, "Well, I'm not trying to say you're wrong, but I believe one hundred percent in Tate. She is honest to the core, which is why I know you will work through this. What you have together cannot be destroyed in three days."

Liza looked out the window and watched the buildings pass. *She's right*, Liza thought. *And I know Tate loves me. But right now, I don't know quite what to make of everything.* "I believe what you are saying," Liza agreed. "But I still want to stay the night at your house."

"Of course," Allie said. "We will curl up on the couch with a glass of wine and discuss any topic other than relationships. How does that sound?"

"That sounds perfect," Liza said, thinking about how certain Allie sounded regarding Tate. "How did you meet Tate?"

Allie smiled. "I actually met her through an ex of mine. They played softball together, and I would watch their games." She laughed a bit. "Tate was the shortstop, and she was quite impressive. She had a girlfriend at the time, and the four of us would hang out after the games and drink beer."

"Really?" Liza said, trying to picture her serious and steady girlfriend all sweaty, drinking beer after playing a game of softball. "I wonder why she doesn't play still."

With a shrug, Allie turned them onto her street. "Well, as fate would have it, our girlfriends ended up hooking up and dumping us, but Tate and I stayed friends. After a while, I think Tate just got a lot more serious about her career. Weekends weren't for playing anymore."

"That sounds like Tate," Liza said. "It worries me that she works so hard." She sighed. "But I don't know that she can change."

WALKING INTO THE EMPTY HOUSE, aside from Zombie sleeping on the back of the couch, Tate's shoulders sagged with sadness. Her life had been turned upside down, and the fact Liza would not be spending the night with her was crushing. "How did I let this happen?" she said to Zombie who did nothing but open one eye. "How did everything get so out of control?" Dropping her bag onto the couch, she sank next to it. It seemed impossible for everything to unwind in less than a week. Closing her eyes, she let her head rest on the cushion, wishing she could simply fall asleep and have everything be a bad dream.

When her phone buzzed in her pocket, she grabbed at it hoping it was Liza. Yet when she looked at the screen, it was the last person she wanted to talk to. Aurora Price. She contemplated not answering but somehow knew the woman would keep calling until she did. *What could she possibly have to say to me*, she thought. *Especially after the way things ended on the sidewalk at the restaurant.* Pushing the connect button, she lifted it to her ear. "Hello."

"Tate," Aurora said, her voice low, and strangely appealing. "Thank you for answering. I'm worried about you." For some reason those words were enough to set Tate off. All her walls to keep out her anger started to crumble. *How can this woman have the nerve to say she is worried about me?* Tate wondered. *After the mess she has made of my life?*

Yet, as much as she wanted to blast her on the phone and

place blame, Tate took a deep breath and let it out slowly before answering. "I'm fine. You don't need to worry about me."

There was a long pause before Aurora answered. "You don't sound fine. Do you want to talk about it?"

"No," Tate snapped before she caught herself. "No, I do not."

"Well, if you change your mind…" Aurora said in a slightly cooler tone. "I'm always here for you." Tate didn't even bother to respond and instead disconnected the call. She wasn't sure what she was going to do about the Aurora Price problem, but right now, she only wanted to talk to one person—Liza.

With the phone still her hand, she dialed her girlfriend's number and waited. It rang four times and then went to voicemail. Tate wasn't surprised, but it did not help her disappointment. "Hi," she said softly. "I miss you. I'm sorry. I know you're safe, but I hope you will also consider coming home." Hanging up, Tate felt a tightness in her throat from the threat of tears. She hated to cry, and it had seemed she was on the verge way too often the last few days. Sitting there alone in the dark, hoping that Liza would call was not going to help and she knew it. *I need to do something to distract myself,* she thought. *I can't just sit here.* Suddenly, the answer came to her. She would go to the place that was almost as special to her as Ruby's—her gym.

A quick change into her workout clothes and she could jog over to the gym and lift weights until her body was so tired that she might have a chance to sleep tonight. *And with a little luck, things will be better in the morning.*

TAKING a long sip of the delicious margarita, Liza relished the flavors of tequila and lime before she swallowed. The alcohol could not affect her fast enough. She felt miserable and wanted any means of escape. It didn't hurt that the cocktail was made by Vivian and therefore one of the best she ever had. The woman was simply a magician when it came to mixology. Liza hummed. "This margarita tastes fantastic," she said. "I don't know what you put in these, but they are always the best."

"Thank you," Vivian said as she sat in the armchair across from where Allie and Liza sat on the couch. "I've been making them for far longer than I willing to admit, but I'm glad you like it."

Taking another sip, Liza sighed as she swallowed. "Please tell me you made it a double though," she said, and Vivian smiled.

"Of course."

For a moment, no one said anything as they enjoyed their drinks and the camaraderie of good friends. Then Allie cleared her throat. "I'm going to guess that you do not want to speak about Tate tonight," she said. "Although we are here to listen to anything you feel like you need to say."

"No," Liza said shaking her head emphatically. "That is the very last thing I want to talk about. Everything is a disaster, and I don't want to focus on it right now."

"Fair enough," Allie said. "That topic is off the table. I imagine you don't care to talk about your upcoming birthday either?"

Liza barked a laugh. "Absolutely, positively not. It falls on the day of the Portland Pride Festival this year so let's just forget about celebrating me."

"We'll see about that," Allie said as she turned to Vivian. "Shall we use the time to talk about our Pride booth? It's only a few days away, and we still have to come up with a right game plan."

Nodding, Vivian crossed her legs. "I want it to be perfect."

"Unique," Allie added. "Not just trinkets and swag with rainbows, but something that makes them flock to the booth." While enjoying her drink, Liza thought about their dilemma. It was nice to let her mind wander in a different direction for a change, and she tried to remember all the different booths she had seen over the years. Rows of them lined up along the Portland waterfront during the festival.

She tilted her head. "Food is always good," she said. "And of course, sex toys."

Allie giggled. "I don't know how we could work those into a Ruby's Bar theme, but I agree, those do draw a crowd."

"And snacks are simply overdone," Vivian said. "Besides, Ruby doesn't really do food." Again, they were quiet, each lost in their thoughts trying to come up with an idea. Liza sipped her cocktail again and realized it was almost empty.

As if reading her mind, Vivian stood. "Finish it and I'll go make you another," she said holding out a hand.

"You are a blessing," Liza said. "I could drink these all night."

Allie sat forward on the couch because she was clearly excited with an idea. "What if we served a cocktail at the booth?"

Vivian sighed. "I wish, but we don't have a license to do cocktails at Pride unfortunately. And it's far too late to try and get one."

Allie nodded, becoming more and more excited. "I know, but what if we made the nonalcoholic kind."

"Mocktails!" Liza said. "Those would be perfect. People would line up to get a refreshing flavorful drink, even if it didn't give them a buzz."

"Do you think so?" Vivian asked, but Liza knew the woman's mind was already calculating the different possibilities. "What would we serve?"

Liza held up her empty glass. "Margaritas, of course. You

could have two or three different flavors. Even if you don't have a chance to blend them, everyone likes a well-made margarita on the rocks."

"That's brilliant," Vivian said, slowly nodding as the idea took hold.

Allie set her drink on the coffee table and clapped her hands. "It is perfect," Allie said. "We can use something other than tequila to give them a bold flavor."

"We'll use a non-alcoholic agave blanco," Vivian said. "It will taste enough like tequila to make people enjoy the cocktail as if it were the real thing." She took Liza's glass from her, and Liza saw inspiration lighting up the woman's eyes. "But not cross any lines or break any rules at the event."

"I love it. I just love it," Allie said. "Best of all, we can dress the booth up to be a replica of Ruby's and have a sign that says, 'Welcome to Ruby's' across the top of our booth."

"Yes," Liza said. "We can bring our second home to the masses."

## 16

As much as she would hate to admit it to anyone, Tate spent the morning literally hiding from Aurora Price. Whenever she wasn't forced to go to a meeting, she intentionally stayed in her office with the door closed. It was so bad, she didn't even go get a cup of coffee from the breakroom. Frankly, the situation was ridiculous, yet Tate couldn't seem to get control of things. Aurora. Liza. Sitting in her office chair, she stared at her computer screen and tried to figure out what had happened to her life. Unfortunately, there were only rows of numbers and dollar signs and no answers.

Looking at the clock, she saw it was almost lunchtime and realized she would have to leave the safety of her office long enough to do two things: go to the bathroom and find food. The latter she could do away from the office so wasn't concerned about being caught by Aurora. *Unless it's in the elevator,* she thought, deciding to take the stairs. Unfortunately, using the bathroom was another story. *I could use one at the deli.* She shook her head. *I can't believe I'm nervous about going to the bathroom. I'm a grown woman, and I don't have to put up with this anymore*. Standing, she squared her shoulders and strode out of her office. Breezing by the executive assistant's desk, she didn't even hesitate when the young woman held up a hand to pause her. "In a minute," she said glancing over her shoulder. So far, the coast looked clear, and she wouldn't miss the opportunity.

Making it to the bathroom and using it without incident, Tate started washing her hands at the sink before anyone came in. She was almost finished when she heard the door open and, looking in the mirror, her heart leapt into her throat when she saw Aurora. As she watched, the woman turned the lock on the main door of the bathroom, and Tate felt the hair on the back of her neck stand up. *This is not good*, she thought and watched the reflection of Aurora walking toward her. A predatory look was in her green eyes. *Oh, definitely not good.*

Although Aurora always dressed impeccably, her outfit today was especially attractive. Almost sensual. The skirt hugged her hips and showed off her legs, and the lightweight blouse had a neckline that dipped lower than was probably a good idea at the office. *She's wearing that for me*, Tate thought. *Does she still think she can attract me?*

"Hello, Tate," Aurora said as she moved to the paper towel dispenser and tore off a sheet before turning to Tate to hand it to her. "I haven't seen you all morning." Reluctantly taking the paper towel, Tate dried her hands while Aurora took another step until her breasts almost brushed Tate's fingers. "For a second there I thought you might be avoiding me."

Tate swallowed hard. "Not exactly," she muttered hating herself for not being brave enough to outright tell her the truth. But the woman was currently her boss, and she didn't want to make her angry. Starting to move past Aurora, Tate saw the woman turning out of the corner of her eye.

She had only taken a couple of steps when she heard

Aurora give a little laugh, low and sultry. "You know Tate," she said. "I love the way you dress. A little masculine, with slacks and button up shirts. I can tell your body is amazing. Someone powerful, which is exactly what I find attractive in a woman."

Hesitating a second from disbelief, Tate could not find words to reply. All she wanted to do was get out of the bathroom. Reaching the exit, she turned the deadbolt to unlock the door and pulled it open at exactly the same time her executive assistant was trying to come in. They nearly crashed into each other. "Oh, excuse me," the young woman said, and Tate stepped aside to let her pass. For a moment, no one moved and then the assistant looked from Tate to Aurora and back, with a hint of curiosity in her eyes. *Damn it*, Tate thought. *She thinks the two of us are hiding something.* It was the worst thing that could happen.

After calling in sick for work, Liza put on the shorts and T-shirt that Allie had lent her. They were a little baggy but considering she had no other clothing except what she wore to work the day before, she was thankful to have it. Wandering into the living area of Allie and Vivian's condo, Liza found Vivian at the kitchen table reading the newspaper. "I didn't know anyone still did that," Liza said, sitting in a chair across from her.

"What's that?" Vivian asked and Liza motioned at the paper.

"Read an actual newspaper. I thought everyone got their news online or TV."

"Well, I guess I'm old school," Vivian said with a little laugh. "I enjoy reading the articles in some sort of logical format rather than quips with lots of shocking graphics. It's quite relaxing."

Liza tilted her head as she sat in a chair at the table. "That actually makes good sense," she said. "Maybe I should try it sometime."

Vivian smiled. "You can have some of the paper now if you'd like."

"I think I'm too distracted," Liza answered with a sigh. "Actually, what I could really use is some coffee. I don't suppose there is any?"

Vivian set the newspaper aside. "I can make you a cup with the French Press unless you would rather go out to the little coffee shop a few blocks away and have something fancier."

"Actually," Liza said realizing it would feel good to be out in the open on a warm summer morning. "I would love that."

A few minutes later, Vivian and Liza were walking along the river toward a few shops nestled together along the waterfront. "This really is a beautiful walk," Liza said. "Thank you. I needed a change of scenery."

Vivian nodded. "Of course. I'm sure it does feel good," she said. "You've been under a lot of stress."

Liza sighed. "Definitely," she said. "This stuff with Tate has been the worst."

Vivian was quiet as they walked another minute before she spoke. "I have only known Tate for a short amount of time. But I've been a bartender for decades, and I have learned to get a good read of people." She slowed and looked Liza in the eye. "I believe Tate is one of the most honest and hard-working women that I've met. Do you really think she is doing something behind your back?"

Liza was a little surprised at Vivian's candor, but then realized the woman's no-nonsense approach was something she appreciated. She thought about the question for a beat. *Am I being foolish over this?* she wondered. *What if I am jumping to all the wrong conclusions?*

Finally, she nodded. "Actually, you're right," Liza agreed. "Tate is honest and hard-working, and I love her. I don't think she's having an affair, but I feel something is going on, and she won't open up to me about it."

They reached the coffee shop, and Vivian paused at the doorway. "Then I suggest patience," she said, and without waiting for Liza to respond, stepped inside. A moment before Liza followed her, she saw a curly-haired, blond toddler with his mother out of the corner of her eye and could not help but watch. *That is what I want with Tate*, she thought. *But what if it never happens?* She hadn't lied to Vivian. She loved Tate with all her heart, but she also wanted to be a mother in her soul. If she really thought about what had happened between Tate and her the last few days, she realized it was less about a possible affair, and was actually about Tate's unwillingness to get married. The real question came down to one thing—would she pick Tate no matter what, or would she choose the path of having children without her? Liza simply did not know the answer.

THANKFULLY, the rest of the day was filled with meetings where, even if Aurora Price was present, there were others to make her behave. It was hard for Tate to focus, and there were a number of reasons why. Not only was the Aurora situation upsetting her, but she could not stop thinking about Liza. She had not answered any of her texts all day, and Tate tried to be respectful and not call her, but with the day nearly over, she couldn't stand waiting any longer.

With the office door closed, she sat behind her desk and dialed Liza's number. After three rings, she was about to give up when she heard the woman she loved say hello.

"Thank you for answering," Tate said in a rush. "I want you to know that I can't stop thinking about you."

"I can't stop thinking about you either," Liza said in a soft voice. "It's been a really rough day."

"Did you go to work?"

"No, I couldn't bring myself to do it, so I called in sick," Liza said.

*I should've done that too*, Tate thought. *I should've found a way to get Liza to meet me and start repairing this.* Tate let out a frustrated breath. "That was probably the right thing to do," she said. "I'm sorry that everything is upsetting you so much." She hesitated, wanting to find the right words. "I need you know there is nothing to worry about between me and my coworker."

"Nothing?" Liza asked. "I don't one hundred percent believe you."

Tate's shook her head. "I promise there isn't anything—."

"I don't think it's romantic necessarily," Liza interrupted. "But it just feels off." There was a pause, but Tate was patient and Liza continued. "Tate, I need you to be completely honest with me. Is there something weird going on between you and this woman?"

At the question, Tate held her breath. She could admit to Liza she was being harassed by Aurora Price. *But what if I'm blowing things out of proportion?* She wondered. *And I'm reading everything all wrong?* The problem at work was something she needed to take care of on her own. "It's nothing I can't handle," Tate said and there was silence on the phone.

"That's not the answer I was looking for," Liza finally said. "I have to go."

"Liza, wait," Tate started but the call was over. Dropping the phone onto the desk, Tate leaned back in her chair and covered her face with her hands. *Why can't I just tell her the truth?* she wondered, but she knew why. Even if Liza didn't hold Tate somewhat to blame, she knew the woman would be angry, and then all hell will break loose. Still, she had to do something about Liza's insecurity, and as she sat there, the reality of what she needed to do was crystal clear. Picking up the phone again, she dialed Allie.

Her friend answered on the first ring "Tate," Allie said. "Is everything all right?"

"Sort of," Tate said with a hint of relief from knowing she was finally making a decision to move her and Liza forward. "I need a favor. What are you doing tomorrow?"

"I have a meeting with one of my clients in Old Town early in the morning, but my afternoon is free," Allie said. "What do you have in mind?"

Taking a deep breath, Tate steadied herself for what she was about to do. "I am going to take the day off tomorrow," she said. "I need you to go shopping with me."

"Shopping?" Allie said, clearly surprised by everything Tate said.

"Yes, shopping," Tate said. "I've made up my mind. I need to buy Liza an engagement ring."

17

As Liza's eyes fluttered open, for the first time that week, she actually felt like everything might be okay. Morning sunlight drifted through the window in Allie and Vivian's cute guest room, and she heard birds singing in the trees around the building. She had a hazy memory of a dream that was fading, and she could not remember the details except that it felt good. One thing did stand out however, and that was Tate. Whatever the dream was about, and she knew it wasn't like the horrible one about her wedding day. It centered around her love for Tate.

Sitting up and rubbing her eyes, Liza looked at the clock and saw she needed to get out of bed if she was going to be in time for work. Yet even though it was for different reasons, Liza thought she would take a second day off. She had plenty of personal time banked and her boss was always telling her and the others to take breaks when they needed one. *And maybe I can use this time to get my life back in order,* Liza thought. *This feels like it could be an important day.* She knew the reason why everything felt so clear at last. She had picked her love of Tate. Late last night, while she tossed and turned trying to make up her mind, the reality she would lose Tate if she kept acting like she had hit her. Thinking what that would feel like finally helped her realize what she wanted in life. She wasn't giving up on the idea of marriage or having a child, but if she had to choose, she would pick the life she had established with Tate. The woman fulfilled her and was more than Liza could ever ask of someone.

*So what am I waiting for?* she wondered. *I should call her and tell her how I feel.* Picking up her phone from the nightstand, she dialed Tate's number. Even though it was still early, Tate would likely have been up for hours. She would either be at the gym, which was what Liza hoped, because that was what Tate loved most about mornings, or already at work. Liza felt a pang of unease when she thought about Tate at work, but she pushed it away. Over everything else, Liza trusted Tate. When her girlfriend didn't answer, Liza was disappointed but not particularly surprised. It was likely she was on the weight bench with Nikki or, worst case, in a meeting. "Tate," she said, leaving a voicemail. "I'm ready to come home and talk. I love you."

Hanging up, she held the phone in her hands, contemplating what to do with the rest of her day. She would go to the house that she lovingly decorated and made a home for them. A special place she shared with Tate. *And take a long hot bath,* she thought. *Finally let this all go.* An idea came to her. "What if I put on something I know Tate likes and go to her work," she said to the empty room. "I'll get there right before lunch and surprise her. We can go out together and find a quiet place to talk at last."

Reaching the gym, Tate saw Nikki waiting for her near the treadmills. The woman grinned as Tate walked closer. "There you are," Nikki said. "You've been skipping our morning routine, and I have been missing my spotter."

Happy to see Nikki, Tate smiled. "I hope to be back on my normal schedule now," she said, appreciating the closeness she felt with Nikki. Even though the woman was witnessing the unfortunate circumstances going on in Tate's life, Nikki never judged. *She's always there for me*, Tate thought. *She's always there for everyone*.

"What do you say we knock out a couple of miles on the treadmill to warm up and then hit the weights?" Nikki asked, turning in the direction of the machines as if she already knew Tate's answer. It wasn't surprising, because the pair often warmed up with a run together. They would go side-by-side on two treadmills while still keeping up an easy conversation, letting their bodies warm before they tested their muscles. It was all part of a process Tate loved. She appreciated everything about going to the gym. The way she could make her body feel—strong and capable of accomplishing anything. *Especially today*, she thought. *When I go buy a ring for Liza*.

Setting a fast pace on the treadmill, they had only gone a minute when Nikki started in with her questions. "So, tell me what's in your head," Nikki said. "Don't leave out any details."

As her heart rate was slowly increasing, Tate laughed. "You have a lot of demands," she said. "But I guess it's only fair. You've been patient all week. Where you want me to start?"

"That's a tough one," Nikki said. "You have a lot going on."

"Tell me about it."

"Right," Nikki said. "I guess first fill me in on how things are with Liza."

Tate increased the speed of the belt beneath her feet.

"Well, we haven't talked much, but today I hope to reconcile that. I'm not going into the office today."

"Whoa," Nikki said glancing over before she increased the speed on her machine to match Tate's. "This is serious. When was a last time you missed a day at work?" Tate had to think before she answered. It had been years since she didn't show up for work. In fact, she had never officially called in sick, and only in a few emergency situations had she missed any unplanned time off at all, but never a full day. *The firm demands a lot of me,* she thought. *And all along I've willing given it, and yet... look at where I am now.*

With a shake of her head, Tate let that line of thinking go, not wanting to ruin the day. "Never," Tate finally answered. "But you know what? It feels really good."

"That's what I like to hear," Nikki said. "What is your plan for the day then?"

At that, Tate smiled wide. "I'm meeting Allie for lunch," she said. "And then I'm going to do something that I should've done a long time ago." She increased her speed a little more and enjoyed the challenge as well as the feel of her body loosening. Blood pumped through her faster as her muscles became warmer.

Nikki followed suit. "Don't hold me in suspense," she said. "Wait… are you…?"

Grinning, Tate loved knowing that her plan for the day would change her life for the good. "Yep. That's exactly what I'm doing," Tate answered. "I'm going to buy Liza an engagement ring at last."

Nikki let out a long whistle. "And the proposal?" Nikki asked. "What's happening there?"

"I'm not sure," Tate answered, knowing that was the one hole in her plan. "I think I'll just wait for the right opportunity."

Nikki ran faster as they closed in on their finish. "Well,

that's fantastic news," she said. "I know this will all the work out for you two. You're meant for each other."

Tate matched Nikki's pace. "Thanks," she said. "That means a lot."

Holding up a finger, Nikki showed that she wasn't finished. "But that leads us to the second question."

At that, Tate felt a churn of anxiety in her stomach because she knew where her friend was going next. "How are things at work with Aurora Price you mean?"

"Yes, exactly," Nikki said. Tate stared at the monitor on the treadmill and saw they were quickly closing in on the last lap.

Thinking of Aurora, she was ready to be done running so she could throw the weights around and let out a little aggression. "Things haven't changed," Tate answered. "Actually, if anything, they got worse."

Reluctantly, she recounted what happened in the bathroom. "You've gotta be kidding me," Nikki said. "This is crazy. We have to come up with a plan."

"I agree," Tate said. "But she's sly and doesn't do anything obvious when people are around. It's only when we're alone." She let out a growl of frustration. "Even though I try to avoid situations, she seems to track me down."

Nikki was quiet as she slowed the belt on the treadmill. "I wonder if that's why she left Chicago," her friend finally said. "Because of something like this."

Tate raised her eyebrows. "That could be entirely possible," she said. "Maybe we should look into that."

"Oh, I will definitely look into it," Nikki said as she stopped. "If there's something to find, I'll find it."

GLOWING from her visit home and dressed in a green skirt and a cream, sleeveless summer blouse she knew Tate liked,

# TOGETHER AT RUBY'S

Liza drove her Subaru downtown. As always, parking near Tate's office was tricky, but as luck would have it, she found a space along the curb near the building's front doors. Taking it as a good sign, she parked and headed for the entrance. Although Liza had hoped to hear back by now, she hadn't tried to call Tate since that morning. *Maybe another call would've been a good idea considering I am about to drop in on the woman out of the blue*, she thought. *But I think this will be fun.* Of course, Liza had no idea if Tate was in meetings or would even be available, but she crossed her fingers. She would simply hope her timing was right, and she could keep the element of surprise. More than anything though, she wanted to see the look on Tate's face when Liza came whisking into her office, all smiles and her heart happy.

Walking through the revolving door and into the lobby, her good day continued as she reached the elevators right as the car arrived. After a pair of men in serious business attire stepped out, she slipped in and pressed the button to go to Tate's floor. *She's going to be so surprised*, Liza thought with a smile. *But I want her to know I couldn't wait to see her.* Humming along with the elevator music, she waited for the empty elevator to climb the multiple flights to Tate's floor.

With her excitement mounting, Liza quickly navigated her way to the executive assistant's desk outside Tate's closed office door. Feeling a little disappointed when she saw Tate was likely in a meeting since the door was closed, she bit her lip. "Hi," Liza said. "Sorry to bother you, but is Tate in a meeting?"

The woman glanced up from her computer terminal. "Oh, hi Liza," the young woman said. "I'm surprised to see you here today."

Finding the response unusual, Liza tilted her head. "And why is that?"

The assistant blinked as if realizing something might not

be quite right. "Well, Tate took the day off," she said after a beat. "She sent an email early this morning."

Not sure she heard the woman correctly, Liza stepped closer. "What did you say?"

"I'm sorry, Liza, I don't mean to get in the middle of anything, but Tate isn't here," the assistant said. Shocked, Liza simply stared. *Took the day off?* Liza wondered. *When is the last time she has done that? And why did she do it today?* Suddenly, Liza's bright day turned darker. Tate had not answered her phone earlier and had not called back after the voicemail Liza left her. Tate wasn't at work. *So, where the hell is she?*

"Thank you," Liza said backing away. "I seem to have made a mistake."

18

After an excellent workout, Tate was ready to go home and take a hot shower. As she walked out of the locker room with her bag, she noticed Nikki was still there. She was in the middle of a conversation with the pretty blonde who worked the smoothie bar. Always friendly, Tate liked her, but from the looks of things, the blonde was very into Nikki's muscles. Tate shook her head. *Leave it to Nikki to always find someone pretty to talk to*, she thought as she walked closer. *But then, nobody can help but like her.* Looking over as Tate joined them, Nikki had a very serious look on her face. "What's up?" Tate asked.

"Honestly, I'm not sure what to make of it," Nikki said. "But Jen here has just let me in on a little bit of a secret."

Tate raised her eyebrows. "Is this a kind of secret I should know about?"

Her comment got a grin from Nikki, even though her eyes still looked serious. "This concerns you quite a bit," she said. "All of us actually."

"So, what is it?" Tate asked, shifting her bag from one shoulder to the other.

"The gym is up for sale," Jen blurted, clearly unable to keep it a secret any longer. "It hasn't been posted anywhere, but we had a team meeting this morning, and Mr. Rizzo told us. He is selling the gym."

Tate's eyes widened. "What? When?" she asked, not liking the sound of what she heard.

"He said as soon as possible," Jen said. "Crazy, right?"

"Wow," Tate said completely taken aback by the news. She looked at Nikki. "Now I understand why you said you didn't know what to make of it. Do you know if it will stay a gym?

Nikki and Jen both shook their heads. "Mr. Rizzo wouldn't confirm that," Jen said.

"Which means anything is possible," Nikki inserted.

Staring at the floor, Tate tried to process the new information. "It could be horrible," Tate said after a moment. The thought her gym, that she loved so much, would be sold to a stranger upset her. Mr. Rizzo was a great guy and kept the place clean, if not particularly modern. *What will I do if they sell it?* she wondered. *There's no other gym in the area I am even interested in.*

Nikki hummed. "You know," she said with a tilt of her head. "If it's for sale maybe you and I could buy it."

Tate blinked as she let the thought roll over in her head. The idea of owning the gym would be a dream come true, but she knew it was only a fantasy. "That would be amazing," Jen added. "You two would be great owners."

Starting to shake her head, Tate knew the idea was impossible. She hadn't worked a decade to build a career and be on the threshold of fulfilling all her dreams only to throw it all away. Especially for something that was such a huge risk. "I'm sorry," Tate replied. "But that's not for me."

For a second, it seemed Nikki was going to argue, but then the woman sighed. "Understood."

"Please keep me posted," Tate said, and Jen and Nikki nodded.

"I'll be sure to keep my ear to the ground," Nikki said with a sly smile. Tate snorted a laugh. She knew her friend would keep her ear to something at least.

She started for the door. "I have to get moving, or I'll be late meeting Allie," she said near the exit. "I'll talk to you later, Nikki."

The tall blonde gave her a wave, and then Tate was out the door walking through the parking lot to her car. Getting in, she tossed her bag into the passenger seat. The news about the gym was more upsetting than she realized, and suddenly she wanted to talk to Liza about it. Tell her of her concerns. If anyone understood how much that place meant to Tate, it would be Liza. *Even though she's mad at me*, she thought. *I think she would care.* Digging through her bag, she couldn't find her phone. Trying not to panic, Tate looked again and then could only hope she had left it at home and hadn't missed any important calls.

As Liza drove in the direction of the gym where Tate always worked out, she used the Bluetooth in her car to call the woman again. It rang four times and then went to voicemail only causing Liza's frustration to mount. "Tate," Liza said trying to keep her voice even. "I'm starting to get worried. Please don't do this to us. Call me. Now." She hung up. For some reason Tate was not answering her texts or phone calls. Worst of all though, she wasn't replying to the voicemails Liza left her. After her heartfelt message that morning, she expected a different response. At least something, even if Tate said she wasn't ready to talk. With no idea where Tate was, Liza could only hope she would find her at the gym. *And I'm not going to think about her being with anyone anywhere else,* she thought with a sinking feeling in her stomach. *I just can't believe she would do that to us.*

Turning the corner, she pulled into the parking lot behind the gym. Unfortunately, Tate's car was not there, but she still wanted to check. Sometimes the woman would run to the gym from their house. As she went in the back door, she immediately saw Nikki standing alone drinking a smoothie at the counter. When Nikki looked over at the sound, her eyes met Liza's. For a second there was a flicker of something Liza couldn't quite recognize. *Almost like she's not very happy to see me*, Liza thought as she crossed the gym. *But why would that be?*

"Well hey, Liza," Nikki said. "Fancy meeting you here. You look great, but not exactly ready to workout. What brings you to the gym?"

Liza stopped and put her hands on her hips. "I think you know why I'm here," she said. "I'm looking for Tate."

"Tate?" Nikki said as if they weren't best friends and was puzzled by the question.

Liza narrowed her eyes. "Yes, Tate. I think you've met." For some reason Nikki looked suspicious. As if she somehow knew where Tate was but didn't want to say.

"Right," Nikki said, plastering on her killer smile. "Did you call her? She's probably at work."

"Nice try, but I just came from there," Liza said. "She's not in today. Amazingly, she took the day off."

Nikki frowned. "Wow. You went there? Why?" The question had a hint of something odd to it. There was clearly something going on, and Liza could tell their friend Nikki knew what it was.

"Nikki," Liza said. "I need you level with me. Do you know why Tate didn't go to work today?

"Uhm," Nikki hesitated. "Sorry, but I can't answer that."

Shocked by the answer, Liza shook her head. "You can't answer that?" she asked. "Why the hell not?"

With a sigh, Nikki glanced away. "Let's just say I have some privileged information I am not at the liberty to share."

Liza nearly stomped her foot in frustration. "I don't like stuff being done behind my back," she said. "This is your last chance to tell me. Where is Tate?"

Moving closer, Nikki gently put her hands on Liza's shoulders. "Liza," she said. "I love you like a sister. You and Tate are both very important to me. But some things I can't get in the middle of, and this is one of them."

Arriving at the deli to meet Allie, Tate felt a mixture of emotions. Thankfully, she had found her phone at home but when she started listening to the voicemails, her heart broke. The first message from Liza had been hopeful and full of promise, but as the morning progressed, they quickly went downhill. After her sweet voicemail, Liza apparently began looking for her, and Tate, without her phone, missed all the calls and texts. For some reason that she couldn't understand, Liza had even gone to the firm looking for her. That was highly unusual, and Liza never visited without setting something up in advance. *So why did she do it?* she wondered. The timing could not have been worse. *And now she's suspicious as hell.*

As she entered the restaurant, she didn't know quite what to do about Liza, but saw Allie waiting for her at a table. Hopefully, her friend would have advice. "Hi," Tate said taking a seat. "Sorry if I'm late."

"You're not late," Allie said with a wave of her hand. "I just finished up early with a client a few blocks over, so it was an easy walk. I haven't been here long."

Tate started to read the menu on the table. "What are you having?"

Allie pointed at the turkey with pickled beets and Havarti cheese sandwich. "I've eaten here before and they have great food."

The anxiety in Tate's stomach made her hesitate to order something as heavy as a sandwich but she knew she had to eat, especially after her workout. "That will do," she said and put the menu back in its holder with the salt and pepper shakers.

Allie was quiet for a moment, before touching Tate's hand. "Tate, I'll be honest, you don't look quite yourself. I know things have been rough on all fronts for you lately, so please, tell me how I can help?"

Tate sighed as she ran a hand over her face, trying to figure out where to begin. "I'm not even sure," she said. "You've seen parts of what's happening between Liza and me."

"I have," Allie said. "But I got the impression from a voicemail from Liza this morning that she was in a better state of mind. Hasn't she contacted you?"

"Oh, she contacted me," Tate said pinching the bridge of her nose. "And you're right, early this morning when she first called and left me a voicemail it was wonderful. She even told me she loved me."

"Okay. That sounds promising. What is wrong now?" Allie said, holding Tate's hand tighter.

Tate shook her head. "Unfortunately, I didn't get the voicemail until it was too late."

"What do you mean?"

Looking at their clasped hands on the table, Tate felt her eyes burn as tears threatened. "I accidentally left my phone at home when I went to the gym this morning. By the time I found it, Liza had come and gone from the house, planning to surprise me at work."

"Oh no," Allie said. "You weren't there."

"Exactly," Tate answered. "And that made Liza upset, so now she wants to know where I am."

"And you haven't told her anything about us going shopping?" Allie asked.

"No," Tate said. "I don't know when I will have another opportunity to take time off work to look for a ring. I want to propose soon, so we must do it today."

Allie leaned back, a sympathetic look on her face. "I see," Allie said. "Having to do it today means you can't tell Liza what you're doing."

Tate nodded. "I can't tell her, but I don't want to lie either. So, I haven't called her back. All I did was send her a text and said I was sorry that I couldn't explain, but she had to trust me."

"What did she reply?" Allie asked.

"She hasn't."

19

Throwing her clothes haphazardly into a suitcase on the bed, Liza was fed up. She was not going to stay another minute in the house until people, particularly Tate, started telling her the truth. The wineglass on top of the dresser threatened to spill when she slammed the dresser drawer, but she picked it up in time and took a hearty swallow. It was her second and she felt the effects already. *Probably because I haven't eaten much for the last three days*, she thought. *But I better slow down if I'm going to Ruby's and help them with prep for Pride later tonight.*

The other option was to take an Uber and go home with Allie and Vivian again. She didn't love that idea. Another night would feel like she was outstaying her welcome, but she didn't know what her options were other than a hotel nearby. *Or maybe an Airbnb?* She wondered. The idea grew on her as she finished stuffing everything into the carry-on suitcase and zipped it closed. Renting a cute place somewhere in the Pearl District would help lift her spirits. *And give me time to figure out what I'm going to do with Tate.* She still could not believe after all her messages, starting with the loving a romantic one and finishing with absolute fury, that Tate had only sent her one text in return. All it did was ask Liza to trust her. *And it did not explain where the hell she was all day.* She wasn't at work and not at the gym. Liza could not imagine where Tate would be if she wasn't at either of those locations. They were her life. The idea Tate was with Aurora Price reared its ugly head, but Liza refused to believe her girlfriend would do it. *Unless she's at Ruby's?* But that made no sense either. *Why would Tate be hanging out there in the middle of a workday?*

Wandering into the living room with her glass of wine, she wasn't sure what to do next. *I could text Allie again*, she thought. *But she's not answering me either.* It was another thing irritating Liza. Allie always wrote back, and the fact she was too busy for Liza hurt. Not that Liza expected everyone to be at her beck and call, but these were dire times, and she needed her friends. She could always text Vivian to find out where Allie was, but Liza didn't want to drag more people into the situation. Breaking up was always ugly. *Is that what is happening here? Tate and I are breaking up?* Taking another drink of her wine, she realized the glass was nearly empty. Liza closed her eyes and sighed. Her life was simply a disaster.

FRUSTRATED, Tate looked through the clear glass at the many different engagement rings available for purchase. They were at their fourth store and still Tate could not settle on any of the options. All the rings were starting to blur together, and she didn't see what she wanted. The salesman lifted one of the rings from under the glass and held it in front of her so it would catch the light. It was a beautiful emerald cut single diamond on white gold. Truly precious but Tate shook her head. "I'm sorry," Tate explained. "But I'll know it when I see it and that's not it."

"Then we will keep looking," Allie said from beside her. The woman had been infinitely patient through the entire afternoon. They had looked over dozens of engagement rings, but, if Tate was being honest, each store had basically the same inventory. Modern engagement rings were simply not that original. *But maybe that's what Liza wants*, she thought. *Maybe I'm making this too difficult.*

After replacing the ring in the display case, the salesman folded his hands. "Is there anything else you would care to look at?" the salesman asked, also being very patient as Tate asked to look at one ring after another and saying no to everything.

Tate ran her hand through her short hair. "No," she said. "But I'm afraid there really isn't any place else I know to look."

The salesman paused before leaning a little closer. "Have you considered looking at heirloom pieces?"

Tate raised an eyebrow as she considered the man's words and glancing at Allie, she saw a hopeful look in her eyes. "An heirloom piece," Tate repeated. "Something unique. Something with history. Where would I find a ring like that?"

The man made a subtle nod of his head. "You're in luck," he said. "There is a store on the corner of this block that sells antiques and other interesting objects of days gone by." He smiled. "They might have the one you're looking for."

Feeling hopeful for the first time in the last few hours, Tate thanked the man and, with Allie on her heels, went to find the antique store. The minute she stepped inside and caught the distinct smell of furniture polish, moth balls, and incense, Tate knew it was the place. Looking around, she took in the room. The space was filled with antique furniture and various treasures, all in a mix that left little room to walk around. One wall was all shelves, crammed with hardbound and leather books. The other wall was lined with glass displays filled with objects from another age. Even various chandeliers hung from the wood beams across the ceiling. Every bit of it reminded Tate of her mother—a unique woman in every way who loved to collect antiques, feeling each piece could tell a story.

As if conjuring her mother from her memories, she heard an elderly woman call to them from across the store. Tate knew it wasn't her mother, but the timber of the voice was very similar. Every part of the place made her feel welcomed and happy. "I think this is the place," Tate said to Allie in a hushed tone.

"I'll be right there," the woman said, appearing through red velvet curtains that probably led to the back of the store where there was even more marvelous inventory. Wearing a long colorful skirt, a modest blue shirt and a shawl held with a broach that looked like a butterfly, she fit in perfectly with the shop. She smiled. "Welcome to my store."

"It's wonderful," Tate said. "I grew up loving antique shops like this."

"Did you? Perfect," the shopkeeper said, her eyes twinkling with delight. "Are you looking for something specific?"

Moving closer, Tate nodded. "I am," she said. "I'm looking for an engagement ring."

The shopkeeper tilted her head. "For a special woman?"

"Yes," Tate said. "A wonderful woman that I want to marry."

Nodding, the shopkeeper hooked her finger at Tate as she walked behind one of the long display cases. "Follow me," she said. "And describe her, so I can show you a ring that will match."

Tate considered her request for a second. *Can it be this*

*easy?* she wondered, as her hopes lifted. "She is beautiful, intelligent, and loving."

The saleswoman paused. "And that sounds like many women that I have met. Surely, she is more unique than that if you love her so much."

Furrowing her brow, Tate thought for a second and nodded. "You're right. She is also exciting and full of life. Whether it's joy or anger, her emotions are always close to the surface. She is the fire to my ice." Tate felt her throat clench with emotion. "And I cannot live without her."

Nodding, the shopkeeper slid open the back of the display case. "Then I have just the ring for you."

After deciding it was best to take an Uber from her house, Liza sat in Ruby's at the bar across from Vivian. Four small margarita glasses full of different colored liquids sat on the counter in front of her. "Now try these," Vivian said. "And tell me what you think." She smiled. "I know you will be honest." Liza looked the woman in the eye and gave her a half-smile in return. Clearly, Vivian knew her well. Liza never held back her opinion on something.

Picking up the first margarita, Liza appreciated the little glass. "This is cute," she said. "And I promise, I will tell you exactly what I think." Liza examined the creamy orange drink. Yellow crystals coated the rim. "What is this? Salt?" She touched it with the tip of her tongue. The crystals were sweet and had a hint of something fruity. "Interesting."

"Does that mean you don't like it?" Vivian asked.

"I didn't say that," Liza said with a shake of her head. "I do like it. It was just unexpected." She sipped and let the small serving of margarita roll over her tongue before swallowing. It was a beautiful blend of mango and what she guessed was pineapple but with a touch of something she could not quite place. "That's not tequila in there?" She found it hard to believe.

Vivian shook her head. "No, it's not," she answered. "It's the agava blanco spirit that I special ordered. It carries a flavor similar to tequila, but it won't make you drunk."

"Well, that's good for Pride tomorrow, but a bit of a shame for me tonight," Liza said, setting down the glass. She very much wanted to keep her buzz going and forget all about Tate. "I could really use a lime margarita on the rocks with double the tequila."

Vivian's eyes searched Liza's face for a moment. "I understand," she said, turning to take a bottle of tequila from the top shelf before she grabbed a margarita glass from under the counter. With an experienced hand, she quickly made the drink and set it in front of Liza.

"Are you going to make me drink alone?" Liza asked with a raised eyebrow.

With a shrug, Vivian poured herself a second margarita. "I suppose not," she said, and held up her glass in a toast. "To a long and healthy life full of love and friendship," she said, and Liza hesitated for a beat before raising her glass as well.

"Okay, I will agree to that," she said, and they sipped just as the door opened. Liza glanced over to see Marty and Rey walking in.

Their eyes lit up when they saw Liza, and together they quickly crossed the bar to give her hugs. "It's so good to see you," Rey said, but there was a look of worry in her dark eyes. "I'm glad you made it here tonight to help us get ready."

Liza sighed. "I can't let my friends down no matter how much of my life is a train wreck."

"Aw, I hope it's not that. It's almost your birthday," Marty said as she sat on a stool. Liza caught the warning look Rey sent her. "Uhm… or is that topic off the table?"

"It's off the table," Liza replied. "I'm skipping this birthday." She truly meant it. In her opinion, turning thirty not only sucked, but doing so while her future was so upside down was a double whammy.

Rey rubbed Liza's arm. "Well, then we will simply enjoy the day on the waterfront together as friends having fun at Pride," she said, taking the stool next to Marty. "Serving what I imagine are these mocktails sitting in front of you." She waved her hand at the colorful drinks. "Do we get to Beta test?"

"That's the plan," Vivian said, setting more glasses on the counter before picking up the pitcher to pour. "Try each and tell me what you think."

## 20

Driving across Portland with Allie on the way to Ruby's, Tate felt a new kind of excitement. After a long day of searching, she had found the perfect ring for Liza. When the shopkeeper of the amazing antique store reached into the display case, Tate held her breath. After seeing so many rings that day, she figured it was her last hope. The woman set a small, red velvet box on the glass countertop. "This is what you want to give to a woman like you described." she said. "She is special and deserves a ring that has emotion."

Tate nodded. "You are right," she said and looked at Allie. "Would you agree?"

With a smile, Allie clasped her hands together. "I do agree with it completely," she said. "Now open that thing before I go crazy waiting."

With a laugh and a tingle of excitement, Tate picked up the box and held it in her palm for a moment, closing her eyes and wishing the ring was the one she was meant to find for Liza. *Let this ring have a history of long, loving marriages,* she thought. *Let it be a ring that protects our love.* Finally, Tate opened her eyes and lifted the lid. Inside was a brilliant round-cut diamond surrounded by smaller rubies. When it caught the light, it almost seemed to glow. A word popped into Tate's head. *Dazzling.* She heard Allie suck in a breath as Tate met the shopkeeper's eye. "It's beautiful," Tate said. "It is exactly what I'm looking for."

The woman's wrinkled face broke into a wide smile. "Of course, it is," she said. "I've had that ring a long time, as if it was only meant for you and your future bride. Have you waited a long time to marry this woman?"

Feeling a faint blush on her cheeks, Tate nodded. "Yes, I have. Hopefully not too long."

Seeing Ruby's neon sign ahead, Tate thought of her words. She had truly meant them. Losing Liza would devastate her, but it might also be her own fault for waiting so long. Hopefully, tonight she would be able to convince Liza to come home. "Tate," Allie started, making Tate look over. "I have to ask you a question."

"All right," Tate said. "I'm ready."

"Well, maybe it's none of my business, but I was wondering what your plan was is around the actual proposal."

At that, Tate sighed. "I wish I knew," she answered. "I had big ideas of taking her away somewhere, maybe back to Hawaii, but for now, I need to focus on getting Liza home with me. And then we'll see what happens." As she pulled into the bar's parking lot, she thought about Allie's question. *What will I do?* she wondered, and then remembered how she felt finding the ring and knew her heart would tell her when the time was right.

WELL INTO HER third margarita and looking forward to the next one, Liza wondered if Tate would show up at Ruby's tonight. Considering she had not bothered to go to work, the woman would have no excuse for not coming to help prepare for Pride tomorrow. *Unless whatever she is doing monopolizes her into the evening*, Liza thought. *It's not like anyone is giving me any information.* Frustrated, she took another sip of her delicious, traditional, tequila-laced margarita and contemplated what to do next. Amazingly, Allie had yet to arrive, and Liza wondered if she was somehow in on whatever it was that Tate was doing. *But does that really make sense? Or am I grasping at straws?*

Deciding she wanted answers, Liza looked for Vivian. She was talking with Kelly, Ruby's usual Friday night bartender, while she made a drink for a customer. Impatiently, Liza waited for her to finish, and once Vivian was done, she waved her over. "Another?" she said pointing at the drink Liza had nearly finished. "Or are you going to take a break?" As Liza contemplated her question, Vivian raised an eyebrow. "There's nothing wrong with switching to seltzer." Liza pursed her lips. After drinking at home and drinking at the bar, she was seriously feeling the effects of the alcohol. *But does that matter? How drunk do I want to get tonight?* she wondered. *And is there any reason I shouldn't?*

Before she could decide and answer Vivian, the door opened. Liza didn't bother to look because the bar was getting busy with the Friday night crowd. People had been streaming in for the last half hour. It wasn't until Vivian's eyes lit up that Liza glanced over her shoulder to see who the woman was looking at—Allie. And Tate was behind her.

Seeing her, Liza's heart raced a little. As angry as she was, Tate still took her breath away. The chemistry between them was undeniable, and as Liza's eyes traveled over Tate's amazing body, stopping at her handsome face, she felt the usual pull toward her. Matching her gaze, Tate gave her a small smile as if looking for encouragement. Liza was about to motion for her to come closer when she remembered Tate not being at work and giving her no explanation.

With a frown, she turned away but not before seeing the look of disappointment on Tate's face as she moved closer. "Do you mind if I sit here?" Liza heard Tate say behind her.

A stool had opened beside Liza and knowing she couldn't stop her, Liza nodded. "You can sit wherever you want," she said. "I don't own this bar."

Not commenting, Tate took the stool and sat very close to Liza. So much so Liza felt the heat from her strong body and the scent of her skin. "I want to talk to you," Tate said softly, the words almost lost as the music started. "Will you come home?"

Liza wanted to go home with Tate. The alcohol was having the opposite effect of what she thought it would. Instead of giving her courage, it was making her sad. Still, she was never one to give in to a fight, and she shook her head. "I'm not ready to come back to you," she said and knowing she couldn't sit next to Tate and keep her resolve, she decided it was time to dance. Sliding off her stool, Liza saw the dance floor was starting to fill and with a look around, she noticed Marty sitting beside Rey in their usual booth. Deciding she needed a partner, Liza wandered across the bar to Marty and Rey. "Can I steal Marty away for a few minutes?" Liza asked, tapping her friend on the shoulder. "I need a dance partner."

"Oh," Rey said with raised eyebrows. "Of course, have fun.

Marty looked part surprised, and part confused, but she was a good friend and gave Rey a quick kiss before following Liza onto the dance floor. Swaying to the music, Liza closed her eyes and tried to let all her conflicting emotions go for a minute. *Just enjoy the music,* she thought. *And forget about everything.* Yet, when she opened her eyes to look at Marty, she saw Rey and Tate had taken a spot beside them. Her eyes widened with surprise because Tate never danced. *She is making an extreme effort to lure me back.* A part of Liza's heart went out to her and before she could stop her emotions, Marty leaned toward Tate. "Want to swap?" Marty asked and Tate nodded. Suddenly Liza was dancing with her girlfriend, the woman she had given her heart to, and she thought was her whole world. Moving closer, Liza let herself be caught up in the moment. As Tate put her hands on Liza's hips, they swayed together in rhythm with the dance music.

For a moment, it seemed like everything was going to be okay. Tate had Liza in her arms, and they moved to the music as one. Although not much of a dancer, Tate put everything she had into that moment. When their eyes met, the instinct to kiss Liza was strong but before Tate could move closer, the woman's eyes grew wider. She put her hands on Tate's shoulders. "No," she said pushing against her. "It's not going to be that easy. I want answers." With that, Liza walked off the dance floor.

Tate swore under her breath. "Liza, wait," she said, following her girlfriend. She expected Liza to go sit in the gang's normal booth but instead she kept going across the bar. *Where is she going?* Tate wondered, ready to reach for her arm and stop her so they could talk.

As if reading Tate's mind, Liza whirled around and put her hand up to stop her. "I'm going for a walk," she said. "Don't follow me."

"Wait a minute," Tate said. "You've been drinking. Let me come with you."

Liza gave Tate a glare. "Suddenly you have time for me?" she asked. "Whatever you have been up to all day is done?"

"Yes," Tate said as patiently as possible. "You are my entire focus."

Liza lifted her chin. "Well, I'm going for a walk. You can do whatever you want," she said, heading for the exit.

Just as Liza reached it, the door opened and in swept Nikki with Jen, the beautiful young blonde woman from the gym, on her arm. "Whoa," Nikki said, almost running into Liza. "What's the rush?"

"I need some fresh air," Liza said, pointing a finger at Nikki. "And don't think I'm not mad at you too."

Nikki raised her eyebrows. "Why me?"

Liza waved her hands around. "Because you're in on this," she said before pushing past them and out of Ruby's.

Nikki's eyes met Tate's. "Is there something specific going on here, or is it still the same thing?" she asked, and Tate sighed as she started to walk out the exit.

"It still the same old mess. But I'm going to walk with her."

Before she could pass, Nikki put a hand on her arm. "I'm not saying you should tell her about what you did today, but you need to tell her the rest. It will help clear things up." Tate thought for a moment about her friend's words. *Maybe she's right*, she thought. *Maybe the right thing to do is to just confess everything to Liza. We shouldn't have secrets like this.*

With a nod, she started for the exit. "I will," Tate said, and then hurried outside to find Liza. The woman was already to the corner and waiting for the light, so Tate jogged in her direction. "Where are we headed?"

"No place in mind," Liza said as the light changed, and she started walking without seeming to care if Tate followed or not.

"Those are the best walks," Tate said. "And this might be just what we need, because I have something that I need to tell you." She put a hand on Liza's arm. "Something I should have told you a while ago."

Liza slowed and looked over her shoulder. "Then tell me," she said. "Please."

Tate took a deep breath. "I hate to admit this actually," she said. "I honestly don't know how it happened, but…"

"What?" Liza asked, exasperation clear in her voice. "What has happened?"

"It's about Aurora Price," Tate said. "I think… no, I know it." She grit her teeth before forcing out the next sentence. "The woman is sexually harassing me, and I don't know what to do about it."

21

With a steady throbbing at her temples, Liza rolled over in the soft bed and let out a little moan. When she bumped into a warm body, her eyes opened. In the early morning light, she saw Tate's head resting on the pillow beside hers and realized exactly where she was—home. She was in their beautifully decorated bedroom in their king-sized bed, and it felt wonderful. *I didn't realize how much I missed this,* she thought. Waking up beside Tate was all Liza ever wanted, and she was sorry it had taken her so long to realize it. After talking with Tate for a couple of hours the night before after they were home, Liza understood so much more. Even through the haze of alcohol, she felt Tate's confusion and pain over Aurora Price, but also the lost promotion, and it made Liza a little crazy.

While they were still on the sidewalk near Ruby's, Liza had wanted Tate's phone. Furious, she had every intention of calling Aurora Price and giving her a piece of her mind. There was no way she was going to let some woman make Tate feel so horrible. Being her usual levelheaded self, Tate asked Liza to calm down and think. "Let's go home and talk about this," Tate had said, taking Liza's hands in her own. "We need to handle this delicately. Aurora is currently the person I'm reporting to, which makes her my boss. I can't accuse her of things I cannot prove."

Liza had wanted to argue, and the alcohol did not help, but she could see the pleading look on Tate's face and so relented. For the moment. She had every intention of discussing it again today, but as she lay in the bed beside Tate, she studied the woman's face. She was still asleep and looked so relaxed Liza could imagine what she was like when she was younger. All the lines of worry were gone, and Liza realized she didn't appreciate how much stress Tate was under all the time. Reaching, she touched Tate's cheek and the woman's eyes fluttered open. Turning her head, their eyes met, and Tate smiled. "Good morning," she said. "I can't tell you how much it means to me to have you here right now."

"It means a lot to me too," Liza said, snuggling closer while Tate wrapped an arm around her shoulders. Liza rested her head on Tate's chest and heard the familiar sound of the woman's heartbeat. "I missed you."

Tate kissed the top of Liza's head. "Thank you for listening last night."

"I should've listened sooner," she said, but Tate shook her head.

"You didn't know."

Liza lifted her head and looked into Tate's face. "I should've pressed harder sooner," she said. "Instead of getting upset like I always do. I should've insisted on the facts instead of jumping to conclusions."

"And I should never keep that kind of secret from you," Tate said.

Liza thought about the woman's words and could not help but wonder about the day before. They still hadn't talked about where Tate was, and she still wanted to know, but she also didn't want to spoil their special moment. Still, she had to clarify one thing. "Tate," she said. "I understand you don't want to talk about yesterday, but can you please promise me it has nothing to do with what is happening to you at work."

"I promise," Tate said and kissed Liza gently on the lips. "And when the time comes you will know everything. I promise."

Liza hesitated for a beat as she looked into Tate's eyes. "I trust you," she finally said and kissed Tate again. Harder and more passionately than before. The heat from Tate's lips on hers sent a warm glow through Liza's body.

Breaking the kiss, Tate ran a hand over Liza's hair. "I want to wish you a happy birthday," Tate said. "I know we are not celebrating, but I need you to know that I remember today is your day.

Liza tilted her head and gave her girlfriend a sexy smile. "There are some aspects of my birthday I wouldn't mind celebrating."

"Oh?" Tate asked with a raised eyebrow.

"I mean I do want one thing from you on my birthday. It's important to keep up some traditions," Liza said shifting her leg over Tate's hips until her body was on top of Tate's. "Don't you agree?"

Tate smiled and wrapped her arms around Liza's body to pull them closer together. "I could not agree with you more."

TATE HUMMED WITH PLEASURE. Slipping from under Liza's body, she swung her legs off the bed and reached for the nightstand drawer. "Is there anything special you want for your birthday?" she asked over her shoulder where Liza still lay under the sheets.

"I think you know exactly what I want," Liza said, her voice having taken on a husky tone. "I want to ride you."

Tate felt her entire body clench with anticipation. A heat bloomed between her legs, and she wanted nothing more than to take Liza right then. Standing, Tate could not move fast enough. "I want that too," she said and in a moment was sliding the straps of the harness over her hips.

Watching her, Liza licked her lips, and her eyes took on a wanting look. "You are so sexy," the woman said, opening the covers to welcome Tate back into the bed. "You have no idea how much you turn me on."

"Let's see," Tate said as she moved to lay on her back. "Come a little closer."

Without hesitation Liza moved on top of Tate's body. The shaft of Tate's strap-on hadn't entered Liza yet, but she knew from the tremble of Liza's body she would not wait long. Running her hands into the woman's hair, she pulled Liza into a deeper kiss, thrusting her tongue into her mouth until the woman moaned with pleasure. Tate loved conquering Liza, making the woman her own. Doing things to her that no one else had ever done. There had never been a lover in Tate's life like Liza. She was sexy, but that wasn't everything that turned Tate on so much. It was the fieriness Tate tried to describe to the woman at the antique store. Liza had a passion that could burst into a raging inferno and consume them at any given moment. That draw was what made Tate want her all the time. She could not get enough.

Breaking the kiss, Tate ran her lips along Liza's chin and then down her neck feeling the woman's racing heartbeat as she nipped at the hot flesh. In response she heard Liza whimper and start to grind her hips against Tate's hard abs. Even through Liza's panties, Tate felt the wetness building. "You are going to need to take these off," Tate growled as she grabbed the thin band of the woman's underwear. "Before I rip them off."

"Rip them off," Liza murmured into her ear. A flash of heat bolted through Tate at the words, and using a strength built over years of working out at the gym, she wrapped her fingers in the fabric and with one quick tug pulled the fabric free.

Liza gave a little yelp of excitement. "Oh God, I want you. I can't wait."

"Then don't," Tate said and lifted her hips until she felt pressure between Liza's legs. She was close to sliding inside the woman she wanted so much. In response, Liza squirmed until Tate felt their bodies connecting. With a moan of pleasure, Liza slid along Tate's body until the tip of the shaft was inside her. "Yes," Liza murmured as she used her arms to sit upright on Tate to straddle her. "Yes, I want you deep. I love it when we do this." Tate knew it was true. Some people didn't understand how two women could enjoy having sex that involved penetration, but there was something special about the connection of two bodies. It wasn't about male or female, but instead, it was about the act of giving and taking. One person letting themselves be vulnerable to another, yet with Liza on top, she held control too. It was perfect.

Pressing down with her body, Liza felt the shaft of Tate's strap-on sliding deeper inside her—spreading her, filling her, taking her body. The sensation was so exquisite she held her breath to savor the moment. Holding her body still, she let herself adjust to the size of the shaft. Even though she had been ready and excited until she could focus on nothing else, Tate's toy was big, and she had to move slowly at first. When Tate put her hands on Liza's hips, she felt the mounting expectation thrumming through the other woman. "Is this what you wanted?" Tate asked, and Liza nodded.

"It is exactly what I want," she said, and she meant it. Somehow, the last few days of turmoil heightened her passion, and the intensity was that much greater. But there was more to the feeling than physical desire. Worrying she might be losing Tate made the moment that much more precious. The connection she felt with her in that moment was everything. Slowly, she started to rock her hips. The movement pushed the shaft deeper inside her, and she let out a moan. "How do you make me feel this way? Why is being with you so perfect?"

"Because I love you," Tate answered and in response she lifted her hips until the shaft could not be any further inside Liza.

"Oh yes," Liza said and started to move her body faster. She lifted and lowered only enough to slide back and forth along the firm sides of the strap-on. "I'm not sure I can take this very long." She already felt the wave building that would take her over the cliff.

"Don't come yet," Tate insisted. "I want more of you." The words drove Liza even crazier, making her squirm with need. When Tate matched the rhythm of her thrusts with Liza's rocking, while using her hands to pull her down harder, Liza threw her head back and let out a cry of delight.

"Please don't stop."

"I'll never stop," Tate said and when Liza didn't think her desire could feel any stronger, Tate moved her hand until her thumb rested above Liza's clit. "Are you ready to explode?" Tate's voice was deep with hunger.

"Please," Liza heard herself whimper. "Please do it."

Clearly not needing any more encouragement, Tate used her thumb to gently slide through the wetness and across Liza's clit. The touch sent a shockwave through Liza, and she moved her hips faster, bumping against Tate's hand. She had many wonderful orgasms with Tate, but this one felt like it would be massive. As Tate continued to circle her clit while Liza continued to rock her hips driving the shaft in and it out, a ripple of ecstasy started from her core. Slowly, as if like molten lava, it burned through her body. When she thought she couldn't take anymore without going crazy, the climax nearly tore her in half. "Yes, Tate, yes," she cried as wave after wave pounded through her. She had never felt more connected to Tate, and Liza knew she was exactly where she wanted to be.

## 22

Driving along Waterfront Park in Portland, Tate noticed a large group of protesters across the street from the entrance to the Pride event. There were always a few picketers in the past years, but what she saw today was almost a mob. "Can you believe that?" Liza asked, looking in the direction of the assembled people.

Tate nodded. "I know," she said. "I've been coming here for years, and it's never been this bad. This is craziness."

After pulling into the parking lot a few blocks from where people stood in line to go to Pride, Tate and Liza hurried in the direction of the entrance. Tate wanted them inside the fence surrounding the park as quickly as possible. As much for their own safety but also to see if everything was all right with Vivian and Allie's booth. There was no telling what might be going on with so much hatred building right outside the entrance.

As they approached the gate, Tate saw a young man with bright green hair, a long, black leather jacket, and studded boots coming toward them on a skateboard. As he flashed past, Tate realized he was headed for the front gate of the Pride event as well. Yet before he could make his turn off the sidewalk and cross the street, one of the protesters stepped from the crowd and tripped him. The skateboard went flying as did the young man until he was sprawled in the closed off street.

"What the hell?" Tate heard Liza exclaim from behind her. "They can't do that." Tate was already in motion.

As the group of protesters gathered around the boy on the ground, she pushed past people to stand protectively over the young man. "Get back," Tate said to the protesters. "What do you expect to do? Are you a lynch mob?"

At her words, most of the group stepped back, but one beefy man, with a bright, red face, a thick, black beard and tight, military haircut, did not budge. "Maybe it's time we start having those again," he said, spitting on the ground. "We need to start doing something before you get even more out a hand."

Tate shook her head. She didn't even have an answer for such ignorance. Instead, she turned to help the boy up just as she saw Liza approaching. The woman's eyes were flashing, and Tate knew there was about to be an encounter. Wanting to stop her progress and avoid an escalation of the situation, Tate tried to step in her path, but Liza would not be denied.

Getting into the man's face, she pointed a finger at his chest. "Out of hand?" she snarled. "Who are you to tell me that I have no place in this world? All we want is our basic human rights. Or is that too complicated for your pea-sized brain to grasp?"

The man's eyes widened, looking shocked by her outburst for a moment but then quickly recovered. "Well, aren't you something," he said with a smirk. "Flying at me like a wet hen all in a rage." He glanced at Tate and then back at Liza. "You don't look like one of them. What the hell is wrong with you?"

"I don't look like one of them?" Liza said, putting her hands on her hips. "If you mean looking like a woman who loves other women, I am most definitely like them." She tossed her head. "I have never been happier than who I am now."

The man snorted a laugh. "Oh, I'm pretty sure I could make you happy."

Tate heard enough and knew things would only get uglier from there. After helping the young man to his feet, she put an arm around Liza's waist and pulled her back. "Let's go," she said, and the man laughed.

"Now isn't that a sight," the man said with danger in his eyes as he stared at Tate. "We got ourselves a knight in shining armor with this little butch." Tate grit her teeth. It was all she could do to not punch the man in the face. He outweighed her by probably fifty pounds, but it looked like he had run to fat, and she knew she could take him. But there were others behind him, and she could not fight them all. Instead, she put Liza behind her and looked the man in the eye. "If you mean I protect my own, then yes, I suppose you're right. We all have each other's back. It's part of who we are and the community we belong to. I doubt you understand though. All you can see is hate."

The man's eyes narrowed, but before he could say another word, Tate saw two police officers approaching out of the corner of her eye. "Break it up," one of them said, but Tate refused to step back. She wanted the ugly man to move first. Staring him down, she saw something in his eyes behind the hate, but then it was gone.

As the cops closed in, he put up his hands and waved them off. "Nothing is happening here," he said and took the step back.

"He's right," Tate said. "There is nothing happening here."

Turning, Tate took Liza's hand, joining the young man with the skateboard, and together they walked away.

Liza had never been prouder of Tate or more furious at another human being. The actions of the protesters were insane, and she wasn't going to stand for it. Even though Tate tried to stop her, she had rushed in and given the man a piece of her mind. But in the end, she was not able to break through his ignorance and instead, they walked away.

As they crossed the street, Liza saw Marty in line. Clearly, she and the entire line had watched the whole thing, and as Liza and Tate approached, they started to applaud. "You have nerves of steel," Marty said once they joined her. "Both of you."

"I'm not sure that best describes me," Liza said, the adrenaline slowly fading and letting her heart rate return to normal. "Tate is the one who is steel. I'm more like a heat seeking missile."

Marty grinned. "Fair enough," she said. "Step in line with me. Rey's already inside helping with setup."

They were almost to the tables where security was checking bags, and Liza pulled her oversized purse off her shoulder to hand to the woman who then searched it. "That could've been real trouble," the guard said as she opened the purse and peeked inside. "They are worse than ever today."

Liza glanced back at the crowd of protesters and nodded. "Yes, they seem to multiply every year, but this is crazy."

"A sign of the times," the woman said handing back the purse.

Once they were through security, Liza, Marty, and Tate wandered the venue until they found Vivian and Allie's large corner 'Welcome to Ruby's' booth. The space was decked out with red and gold neon lights, a disco ball, and plenty of rainbow flags. Dance music played from a small speaker, and hanging from the most prominent corner was a lit Ruby's bar sign, a perfect replica of the one that stood outside the actual bar. "This is fantastic," Liza said, taking in everything with wide eyes. "I can't believe you pulled all this together so fast. You've totally outdone yourself."

"Do you think so?" Allie asked. "I won't lie, the last twenty-four hours have been crazy.

Feeling a pang of guilt for not helping more, Liza nodded. "It really is amazing. There's not another booth like it."

"That's what we are aiming for," Vivian said with a wide smile. "And here comes a large group, so everybody, man your stations. Or women them in this case." With a laugh, Liza did as instructed. Tate stood beside her ready to serve mocktails. Taking a last look around at the booth, Liza noticed that they weren't all there. "Where's Nikki?"

"She let me know she was running a little behind schedule," Tate said. "Late night."

Liza rolled her eyes. "Why am I not surprised," she said and couldn't help but wonder why her friend always needed a different woman every weekend. After their rough week, Liza was thankful she could wake up next to Tate every day. A woman she loved and knew loved her in return.

WORKING at her station Tate helped to serve the mocktails, loving all the energy of the growing crowd. People were crazy about the margaritas Vivian had concocted. A line formed, and it wasn't even noon. While she was chatting with one of the customers who had not heard of Ruby's bar, she noticed something odd out the corner of her eye. Glancing, she saw a man dressed in a suit complete with a tie and dress shoes. He could not look more out of place but was clearly interested in the 'Welcome to Ruby's' booth. *What is that guy doing here?* Tate wondered, not feeling threatened, but curious. *It's like he wandered in here by accident. And why does he care about us?*

Before she could think about it further, she saw Nikki wandering through the crowd with a large rectangular box in her hands. When she saw Tate, she smiled. "I found you," she said. "What an awesome looking booth."

Tate smiled back. "Glad you could make it," she said, and Nikki winked.

"Well… I was up a little late last night," she said. "And maybe up a little early this morning too." The comment made Tate recall her morning with Liza, and she felt a bit of heat run through her. Their lovemaking had been amazing, amplified by the scary week they had. "Now what are you thinking about?" Tate heard Nikki ask. "Please tell me you had a great morning too."

Tate felt a blush rise up her cheeks at being caught, but it didn't keep her from giving her friend a quick nod. "Let's just say things have significantly improved," she said and as Nikki swept into the booth past her, her friend leaned closer and whispered in her ear.

"Nothing could make me happier."

Then, with a sudden flourish, Nikki set the box on one of the tables in the booth. "What is that?" Liza asked as everyone turned to look.

"Well, Liza," Nikki said. "I figured since you were already mad at me that I might as well bring you a birthday cake."

"A birthday cake?" Liza asked as Tate studied her face to see what kind of reaction she would have. When Nikki suggested surprising Liza, Tate hadn't been sure, but when everyone else in the group text agreed with Nikki, she went along.

Nikki opened the box to display a beautiful white cake with colorful roses forming a rainbow across it and *Happy*

*Birthday, Liza* spelled out in cursive on top. "Okay?" Nikki asked. "You don't think we could let this special day go by with no celebration, do you?"

Clasping her hands together, Liza's eyes glistened. "Thank you all so much," she had. "I didn't think I wanted a cake, but this is so beautiful…" She reached for Tate's hand. "This really does mean the world to me. I love you all." Rey, Marty, and Allie all gave her a quick hug before rushing back to serve the waiting crowd.

Liza looked at Nikki. "I imagine everyone is in on this, but you instigated it didn't you?"

The tall blonde woman shrugged. "Maybe. Now, how about we sing happy birthday?"

"That's not really necessary," Liza said, waving her hands. "I'm fine—"

Before she could get out the rest of her sentence, Nikki started singing. All the others quickly chimed in and they serenaded Liza with the familiar song. People waiting in the lines and gathered along the tables started to sing as well.

As she sang, Tate could tell what was happening was a magical moment for the woman she loved and stepping closer as a song finished, she took Liza in her arms. "Happy birthday, Liza," she said. "You are beautiful."

## 23

After having a slice of the delicious, raspberry filled, birthday cake, Liza worked the 'Welcome to Ruby's' booth between Tate and Nikki. Business was good. People lined up to have a chance to try the little mocktails. "This is going so well," she said to her friends. "Vivian will get so much more business from this."

Tate and Nikki both nodded. "She is a savvy businesswoman," Nikki agreed. "But I hear you were in on the original idea."

"Really?" Tate asked from the other side of Liza. "Why am I not surprised? You're always creative."

Liza gave Tate a smile before pecking her on the cheek. "Thank you," she said. "But it was a combination of all three of us. Allie and Vivian are the ones who made it actually happen."

Nikki grinned as she poured another row of mocktails to hand out. "You know who else could be an amazing businesswoman?"

With a frown, Liza shook her head. "No," she said, not sure who Nikki referred to.

"Tate."

Surprised, Liza glanced at Tate who apparently had not heard Nikki. *Or she's pretending not to have,* she thought, handing out drinks while telling people to come visit Ruby's. *So, what is Nikki talking about?* Liza was about to ask Nikki to explain when she caught Tate giving Nikki a small shake of her head. "Wait a minute," Liza said. "What am I missing here? Is this another thing that I haven't been told about?" The last sentence came out with a little more bite than she intended, but some of the original anger lingered.

Clearly seeing the change on her face, Tate held up a hand to pause her. "It's not what you think," Tate said. "Nikki is just playing around, right Nikki?"

After winking at a pretty girl in her line, Nikki looked over. "If you say so," she said with a grin. "But you know we would be awesome."

"How would you be awesome?" Liza said, giving them both a glare. "Somebody tell me right now!"

Tate sighed. "She's talking about the gym. It's going up for sale."

"Oh no," Liza said as they information registered. Tate had to be so disappointed. The woman loved going to that gym and had been since before Liza even knew her. "When did that happen?"

"We just heard about it this week," Nikki said.

"That's horrible news," Liza said, still dealing with her surprise.

Tate shrugged. "It is what it is."

Suddenly, Liza thought about what they were saying a minute before. "How does this translate to being a businesswoman? Are you two buying the gym or something?"

"Like I said," Tate answered. "Nikki was just playing around." Not satisfied with the answer, Liza continued to serve mocktails. She would let it go for now but planned to ask Tate about it later. Clearly changing the subject, Tate nodded toward a man in the crowd. "What do you think his story is?"

Liza followed her gaze. There was a stranger wearing a business suit, looking uncomfortable in the summer heat. "That's weird," she said. "Maybe someone should go talk to him." She looked at Tate and smiled. "I think it should be you."

Not sure she heard right, Tate raised an eyebrow. "So why exactly do you want me to go?"

Nikki and Liza both smiled at her. "He looks like a deer caught in headlights," Nikki said.

"Exactly," Liza added. "If Nikki or I go rushing up to him, he'll get spooked and who knows what will happen."

Tate snorted a laugh. "You make him sound like some kind of rare species."

"Well look at him," Liza said. "Don't you think so?"

Still not convinced she was the best choice, but knowing Liza and Nikki were impossible to argue with, she picked up a mocktail. "Fine," she said, walking around the table to exit the booth. "I hope I don't get bit." As she neared him, the man acted exactly like Nikki and Liza said he would—shocked. Then his eyes settled on the drink she held. Tate smiled as warmly as she could muster. "You look thirsty. And I thought you might want to try one of these?"

The man nodded and took the mocktail from her hand. "I wasn't quite sure how to approach."

"Well, you can try one now," Tate said and watched as the stranger took a sip. His face showed delight. Tate's smile widened. "Pretty amazing, isn't it?"

He took another sip before nodding. "It's splendid," he said. "I have never tasted anything quite like it."

"Exactly," Tate said. "That's what Ruby's is all about. Being unique while giving people what they want."

"I see," the man said. "Did you make these cocktails?"

Tate held up a finger. "They're not cocktails," she said. "No alcohol. These have great flavor, but they can't get you drunk."

The stranger nodded. "That's another reason why I'm interested. But you didn't answer my question, did you make these?"

"Actually no," Tate said. "That would be the dark-haired woman over there."

She pointed in Vivian's direction who was chatting with half a dozen eager customers. They all looked enthralled by the dynamic woman, and Tate was not surprised. Vivian knew how to handle a crowd. "Let me introduce you," Tate said, and the man hesitated.

"Are you sure it will be okay?" he asked. "She looks rather engaged."

"I think it will be all right," Tate said, walking in the direction of the booth. She glanced over her shoulder to make sure the man was following. "I didn't catch your name."

"Charles Walker."

"Nice to meet you, Mr. Walker. I'm Tate Nilsen."

"You as well and thank you," Charles said. "I appreciate you coming to rescue me."

As they approached the table, Vivian looked at them. She raised an eyebrow at Tate's companion. "Vivian, this is Charles Walker," Tate said. "He is curious about what we are serving."

"Okay," Vivian said, looking at Charles. "Would you like a mocktail?"

"I actually already sampled one," he said and held up his empty margarita glass. "But I would certainly like to try another flavor."

Vivian looked Charles up and down clearly appraising him and his business suit. "Certainly," she said and poured a soft, orange-colored liquid into his glass. Tate knew it was mango and her personal favorite. "Give this one a try." The man took the glass and while he sipped Vivian's eyes met Tate's. Tate gave her a half shrug. *Don't look at me,* she thought. *Liza and Nikki made me go get him.*

Charles smacked his lips. "This is even better than the other one," he said. "And you make this mixture yourself?"

"I do," Vivian said, and the man shook his head clearly amazed.

"It's an interesting combination of flavors," the man said. "And amazing there's no alcohol in it."

Vivian gave him a slight smile. "Well, that's the trick now, isn't it?"


LISTENING to the stranger express his delight over the mocktails, Liza glanced from her spot in the booth to take a closer look. The business suit was not cheap nor were his now dusty shoes. The blue and red striped tie put the whole outfit together perfectly. *This is not your average businessman. What the hell is he doing at our festival?* she thought, knowing it was time to find out. When there was a pause in her line, Liza stepped closer to Vivian. She looked Charles in the eye. "What brings you to Pride this Saturday?" she asked. "Don't take me wrong but…" She waved at the crowd. "You don't quite fit the pattern."

Charles glanced around and chuckled. "You have a very good point," he said clearly not taking offense. "I've actually never been to a Pride Festival. And although I very much support the LGBTQ+ lifestyle, I have been married to my wife for over forty years." Liza smiled. The man had a lot of charisma, and she instantly liked him, which was not always the case with strangers.

After pouring the man a different flavored mocktail, Vivian held it out to him. "Then why exactly are you here?"

"Actually, I came from a business meeting," he said, pointing at a large building nearby. "Right across from the event." He smiled. "I try not to work on the weekends anymore, but the Japanese investors came a long way to talk to me, so I made an exception."

The answer did not quite satisfy Liza's curiosity. "You saw the festivities from across the street and just decided to check it out?"

"Precisely," Charles said. "I was also a little put off by the protestors. I wanted to show my support so walked right by them to enter here."

Liza's saw Tate nod. "They are certainly out of control."

"Yes," Charles said, looking at Tate. "And I will say you were quite brave. I could see you from down the block and witnessed the altercation. Standing up for your rights is never an easy thing to do."

Tate lifted her chin. "I wasn't only standing up for my own rights. I was standing up for my friends too."

The man's face looked solemn, and he gave her a nod. "Even more admirable."

"But that doesn't quite answer the whole question," Liza said not giving up on finding out the story behind the stranger in the business suit. "Why were you staring at our booth?"

His smile returning, the man chuckled. "Was I that obvious?"

Tate and Liza both nodded. "It was," Liza said. "Which is why we sent Tate to talk to you."

"I see," Charles said. "It's not anything specific that led me here. I walked around and saw all the different booths but was drawn to this one because of the crowd." Liza nodded but didn't interrupt. "I saw people's reaction to what you were serving and at first I thought it was actual cocktails, hence their popularity."

Vivian held up a finger. "But they are not cocktails."

Charles's eyes twinkled. "So I found out. I asked a gentleman as he passed what exactly he was drinking, and he said it was an amazing virgin margarita." Charles set his glass on the table. "So let me ask, do any of you actually own Ruby's bar?"

"I do," Vivian said. "It's not far from here. I bought it just over a year ago, and it's been remodeled by my partner—Allie Dawson.

Apparently, hearing her name, Allie ducked over for a second. "What did I miss?" she asked, and the man glanced at her before looking directly at Vivian.

"I'm in a conversation with this amazing woman who is clearly creative and knows her business," he answered. "May I ask your name?"

"Vivian Wade."

"Perfect," Charles said, holding out his hand. "Vivian, we should talk more. My job is to take creative ideas like yours and make them international sensations."

Vivian returned his gesture. "I'd be interested in hearing more about what you are thinking."

"Then let's talk. What is the address of your bar? I want to come visit," Charles said. "Because I have a feeling you and your mocktails are exactly the thing my investors are looking for."

## 24

"Can you believe how amazing this weekend was?" Liza said as Tate steered them into the garage. "It was crazy how people lined up to have Vivian's mocktails."

Tate nodded. The booth had been an overwhelming success, and Ruby's name had spread amongst all the festivalgoers. She wouldn't be surprised if the number of people coming to Ruby's going forward would be greatly increased.

Tate turned off the SUV. "And then there was Charles," Tate replied. "I mean it's one thing to be successful on a small scale, but if he could somehow bottle Vivian's mocktail recipes and market them like he seemed to think he could..." She shook her head. "Vivian's financial concerns would be over."

"She deserves that," Liza said as they got out of the car and walked to the back door. "I love that Allie found her. They're so good together."

Before they went inside the house, Tate paused and took Liza's hand. "Like we are?" she asked, trying to make it sound playful, but there was an edge of seriousness in her question.

Liza looked at Tate and their eyes held. For a second, Tate wasn't sure what to think, but then Liza leaned in and kissed her on the lips. It was gentle and loving.

"We are an amazing couple," she said. "Now, let's have a glass of wine, sit on the couch and relax. Standing so much these last two days has been hard on my feet."

"Your feet?" Tate asked as they walked into the kitchen and Liza took down two glasses. "Then could I interest you in a foot rub?"

"Oh, you so could," Liza almost moaned. "I'm going to take you up on that."

Tate took the cork out of the wine and poured them both a serving. "It's the least I can do," Tate said. "I feel bad that your birthday fell on Pride this year, and we didn't truly get a chance to celebrate it." She handed Liza her glass. "I would have liked to take you away somewhere special since it's a significant birthday."

Liza shook her head as she walked toward the living room with Tate following. "This is not a birthday I really wanted to celebrate."

Tate had heard Liza say that repeatedly, and it was the reason why she had been so subdued around the birthday celebration. In fact, Liza had basically made her swear she wouldn't do anything out of the ordinary. Tate had complied but wished she hadn't. Liza had reacted with positive emotion over the birthday cake Nikki brought, and Tate realized she may have made a mistake.

Sitting on the couch, Tate sighed. "Still, I'm sorry that I didn't do more."

"It's fine. You did what I asked," Liza said as she set her wine glass on the coffee table and lay back against the cushions. "You can make up for it with one of your amazing foot rubs."

Tate smiled and went to work. As she started to knead the tight feeling out of Liza's foot, she suddenly had a question she hadn't really contemplated. "Liza, I know turning thirty is a big deal for a lot of people, but it seems especially so with you." She hesitated and waited for Liza to comment, but when the woman stayed quiet, she continued. "Why are you so against turning thirty?"

Liza sighed and gave a little shake of her head. "I don't expect you to understand," she said. "You have no problem celebrating your birthdays. But it is different for me."

After considering her words for a moment, Tate nodded as she continued rubbing one of Liza's feet. "You're right," she said. "I have no problem growing older."

"And that's the difference," Liza replied. "I'm afraid."

FEELING TEARS BURN HER EYES, Liza swallowed hard as she thought about her statement. She was afraid of growing older. There were a lot of reasons, and she wasn't sure if she could express them all to Tate.

"Can I ask why?" Tate asked, doing an amazing job rubbing Liza's feet.

"Well, it's not simply a vanity thing," Liza said trying to make the conversation a little lighter. "Although I do want to keep my youthful appearance, so you'll stay interested."

Tate tilted her head. "Babe," she said. "I will always be interested." Somehow Liza knew that was true. The last week was craziness. Even when she thought for second that Tate might be interested in another woman, deep down Liza knew that wasn't the case. Tate would never cheat, of that she was certain, and she honestly believed the woman loved her unconditionally.

Tears threatened again. "Thank you," Liza said. "I love you

so much." For a second she hesitated to bring up a topic that she knew was sensitive. It was deep and emotional, and it might not be the right time. *But then Tate did start this*, Liza thought. *Maybe this is the opportunity I have been looking for.* "It's also because I am afraid I will soon be too old to have children safely. I know thirty is not a cut off like it used to be. But I want to make sure I start young enough to maybe have more than one." Tate was quiet as she focused on Liza's feet while she worked. There was a long minute of silence, and then the woman looked at her.

Liza saw a mixture of emotions but the one that surprised her was fear. "Liza," Tate finally said. "Maybe I should explain a little more about how I feel." She hesitated, but Liza watched her take a deep breath to continue. "You have mentioned having children since we met, and I have never said that I don't want them. It never occurred to me you worried about getting too old for it, but now I think I understand."

"Do you?" Liza asked, her heart filled with hope.

Tate nodded. "Yes," she said. "But there's more. I think having children would be an interesting experience. The problem is, I'm not sure I'd be a good parent."

Nothing could have surprised Liza more. "Why?" Liza asked. "You're the most loving and gentle person I know. You're smart and you're funny, and I think you'd be a great mom."

A small smile broke out on Tate's face. "Thank you for saying that," she said. "But I have very high standards to live up to. My parents were probably the best a person could have." She moved to Liza's other foot. "I'm lucky. I never ever doubted their love, and I always knew they would support me."

Liza considered Tate's words. She had to agree that Tate's parents were wonderful people, and she was very fond of them. The stories Tate told of growing up were warm and entertaining. All those facts did not, however, mean they were impossible to live up to or even if they should try. *We need to build our own memories and traditions,* she thought. *And not worry about anyone else.*

"Tate, I'm just going to say this, and I don't mean to hurt your feelings," Liza said. "But you are a perfectionist. I have always seen that."

Tate raised an eyebrow. "I'm a perfectionist?"

"Yes," Liza said. "If you think about it, you would agree.

Looking into the distance, Tate was clearly considering her statement. "You're right," she said with a sigh. "It's always been a problem with me. I've always wanted to be the best at everything—sports, school, work. It's what drives me so hard."

"I know," Liza said, pulling her feet away and sitting up to slide closer to Tate. "But you don't have to be perfect. Especially not for me." She took Tate's hands. "Don't let that stop you, I mean, don't let that stop us from having a family of our own."

Tate put her arms around Liza and pulled her close. "I will try," Tate said. She kissed Liza and then pulled back. "Hold on a second."

"Where are you going?"

"I'm going to get something," Tate replied and started across the room when her phone rang in her jeans pocket. Acting instinctively, she pulled it out. Liza watched her whole body stiffen when she saw the screen.

Liza raised her eyebrows. "Who is it?" With a sigh, Tate held the screen so Liza could see the name on it. Aurora Price.

. . .

KNOWING there was no way she was going to answer the phone in the middle of going to the bedroom to get Liza's engagement ring, Tate tossed it on the coffee table. "Wait," Liza said. "Will she leave a voicemail?" As if in answer, the phone chimed, letting Tate know Aurora had left something. She was sure she did not want to know what it was, but Liza was clearly curious. "I want to listen to it." Tate hesitated. She had thought the moment was right to propose to Liza after their conversation about children but now the moment seemed to be spoiled. *Because of Aurora Price again*, she thought. *That woman keeps screwing up my life.*

"All right," Tate said returning to the couch to sit next to her.

She opened her phone and pressed the voicemail button. "Tate, Tate, Tate," the sexy voice of Aurora Price said from the phone. It was low and sultry and in Tate's opinion, there was no mistaking it was not officially business.

She almost wanted to end it then and reached for the phone, but Liza waved her off. "I want to hear this."

"Where have you been?" Aurora purred. "I have missed you... because I have so many *business* questions to ask you." *She's clever*, Tate thought. *She's not going to say anything that I could use against her.* "Call me. I'll be up all night."

The call ended and Liza sprang to her feet. "I am going to kill that woman," she said, starting to pace the room with a furious look on her face. "How can she be doing this and getting away with it?"

"It's because she doesn't say anything directly," Tate replied. "It's all intended for me to read between the lines. She is very smart."

"Oh no," Liza said. "If she was smart, she wouldn't be messing with my girlfriend. I'm going to put a stop to this."

Tate stood and stopped Liza from pacing. She gently took her hands. "You can't do anything," Tate said as calmly as possible. "There is no proof, and without proof, it's my word against hers." She swallowed hard. "And I'm not sure that would hold up."

Liza blinked. "Why not? You've worked there for a decade, and they know how honest and dependable you are."

Tate nodded and hated what she had to explain next, but she needed to make it clear to Liza that storming into Aurora's office and confronting her would not help matters. "A few days ago, Aurora trapped me in the bathroom."

"She what?" Liza spat. "Does that mean—?"

"No, no, no," Tate said, shaking her head. "It's not like you're thinking. She just came across as suggestive. She stood too close to me, handed me a paper towel and let her hand linger. And…well, she said she liked the way I dressed. Masculine. Just the way she liked."

"Unbelievable," Liza said. "But I still don't understand why that puts you in jeopardy."

Tate's stomach tightened with anxiety. "Because when I came out of the bathroom I ran straight into my executive assistant, and she saw Aurora in the bathroom over my shoulder. I'm sure I looked flushed, and I am sure Aurora was smiling. "

"Which could suggest that something consensual might've been going on," Liza finished.

"Yes," Tate said, and Liza threw herself on the couch.

"I don't care. We can't let this keep happening," she said. "We need proof." She sat up straighter. "Like you record her on your phone in a meeting or something."

"Maybe," Tate said thinking it through. *That could be a possibility*, she thought. *I could have a meeting with her and hide my phone somewhere where it could hear us*. She started to nod. "I will try that."

"Good," Liza said, shaking her head. "Where did this woman even come from?"

"Chicago," Tate replied. "Nikki said she would look into her background a little more, but she hasn't told me anything."

"There must be something," Liza said. "But at least Nikki's on it, and if anyone can find out the dirt on this woman, it will be her."

## 25

Arriving at the gym, Liza was crossing the room to the elliptical machines when she felt someone come up beside her. Turning to look, she found Tate with damp hair and a wide smile. "Good morning," she said. "I love it when we can work out together."

Liza tilted her head. "We didn't exactly work out together," she said with a playful smile. "You've been here over an hour already."

"True, but I like that we share this gym."

Reaching, Liza fixed Tate's collar. "And it's always nice to run into you after you've just come out of the shower in the locker rooms," she said. "And all dressed up for work."

Tate ran a hand through her hair. "I'm glad you think so," she said and then her face fell. "I hope we can find a new place if this one closes."

"Is that what will happen?" Liza said with a frown. "Won't it just change ownership?"

After leaning in to give Liza a quick kiss, Tate shrugged. "Who knows? No one is talking about it." She sighed. "My gut tells me the place won't be the same no matter what happens."

"Let's simply wait and see. It might all work out for the best," Liza said. "I'll meet you at Ruby's tonight?"

Lifting her bag's strap to her shoulder, Tate nodded. "Absolutely," she said. "We deserve to have a little celebration over how well things went this weekend."

Liza smiled. "Yes, we do," she said. "So don't be late, dear."

With a chuckle, Tate started for the exit. "I promise this time I won't be."

Suddenly, Liza realized Nikki wasn't around. As Tate's normal workout partner, it was rare for her to skip a morning. There was no way she would miss chitchatting with Liza. Whenever she made it to the gym before work, her friend was almost always there. "Tate, where's Nikki?" she asked, with a glance toward the weights.

Tate frowned. "You know, she hasn't been here at all this morning," she said. "I am surprised because this weekend she talked about a new lift she wanted to try.

"Did you text her?"

"I did," Tate said. "But she hasn't answered yet."

Liza hummed thoughtfully. "I guess we shouldn't worry too much," she said, remembering the many times Nikki disappeared for a few days, usually without anyone knowing where she went, although she at least told one of them she was going to be gone. "I'll text Allie and Rey later and see if they have heard anything."

"Let me know," Tate said. "I'm sure it's fine. You know Nikki. She'll be back when she's back. See you tonight."

Watching Tate go, Liza could not help but notice there was a change in her girlfriend this morning. Even with her concern about the gym being sold, and wondering about Nikki, she seemed more at ease. *More like the Tate that I fell in love with,* Liza thought, realizing it had been a long time since she had seen Tate relaxed. *She's been under a lot of pressure. Maybe our talk was even more important than I realized.*

Climbing onto the elliptical machine, Liza rearranged her towel and her water bottle before pressing the buttons to start the pedals in motion. *It really was a good talk*, she thought. It seemed like for the first time her message really got through. Not that it was Tate's fault. Liza understood she was never direct enough, never explained she was afraid of not having time to have children. After last night, Tate truly seemed to hear Liza, and she was reassured they would work something out.

For the first and hopefully last time, Tate wanted to see Aurora Price. Unfortunately, opportunities to be alone with her did not happen. Even though Tate went to work with every intention of finding time alone with the woman, whenever she tried to approach Aurora, there was always someone else present. So far recording her saying something inappropriate wasn't working. *Could she possibly know I have a new agenda?* Tate wondered. *That would be impossible. She's smart, but she's not a mind reader.* With nothing but group meetings on the calendar blocking out the rest of her day, it was unlikely Tate would get the chance she was looking for. *I will have to try again tomorrow.* She sighed. *I hate this, but it needs to be done. Aurora has got to go.*

Walking down the hall toward the main conference room for her first of many afternoon meetings, she sensed someone beside her. "Where have you been hiding?" Aurora murmured in a sultry whisper. "I've been thinking about you all morning." Glancing around, Tate was disappointed to see there was no one nearby. No one could overhear something so inappropriate. When Tate didn't answer, Aurora lightly bumped their shoulders in what would easily be interpreted as a friendly way to any onlooker. Tate knew the contact was far from innocent. The woman wanted her attention. "I can't believe you didn't call me all weekend. I really wanted to talk to you, especially last night."

Tate slowed her steps and looked at Aurora with disbelief. The woman seemed to think she was invincible. That she could say anything. Finally, she had enough, and even though Aurora was currently her boss, and fighting her could be a bad career move, Tate was done being toyed with. "I don't want you to be thinking about me at all," Tate said under her breath. "It makes me uncomfortable."

Aurora's eyes widened with surprise and then irritation. "Tate," she said. "I hope you didn't misinterpret anything."

"I don't think I did," Tate replied, starting to walk again. "But regardless, just stop." Aurora narrowed her eyes, moving to follow, but didn't make another comment the rest of the way to the conference room. The space was half filled with men and women in suits, and the meeting was scheduled to go for three hours. It was the monthly financial status update, and in the middle she would give a fifteen-minute presentation about her department. Unfortunately, when Aurora slipped into the seat next to hers, Tate knew it would be hard to stay focused. Scooting closer as if to make more room for others, Aurora turned until their knees bumped. Tate had to force herself not to react. All she did was shift her leg away as her boss started his introduction.

As one person after another went on and on about facts and figures, Tate let her mind wander to last night's conversation with Liza. Liza had been right. Tate was a perfectionist and was letting it stop her from doing something scary. Having children would make Liza truly happy. *And what about me?* she wondered. *Will it make me truly happy?* She had amazing parents and could use them as role models. *I could give a child that same kind of love.* Filled with warm thoughts,

Tate smiled and refocused on the meeting when at the same moment she felt a foot slip under the cuff of her dress pants and caress her leg.

TAKING calls at her desk in the insurance office, Liza tried to remain positive. Even though it was a Monday, and barely after lunch, she was ready to call it a week. People seemed especially irritated. *I wonder if it's a full moon or something,* she thought. *Everyone is so grumpy.* The last customer had been frustrated over what was and was not included under his home insurance policy. Unfortunately, the flooded basement only partially qualified for coverage. She had explained as nicely as possible the conditions of his policy. In the end, he hung up angry, but at least he hadn't called her names.

As her desk phone rang again, she hoped the next person would at least be polite. Before she clicked connect, she heard her cell phone buzzing in her purse. Knowing she couldn't really check it during work hours, Liza ignored it. Connecting the work call, she started in on her greeting. "This is Barbara Wilson's office. My name is Liza. How may help you?"

"Hello," a woman's voice said. "I'm interested in taking out an insurance policy on a piece of jewelry. I have a diamond necklace that I received as an anniversary gift."

"All right, I can help you with that," Liza answered, turning to her keyboard and checking the woman's phone number against their records. There were no matches, so Liza started her new client routine. "What is your name?" The woman started to answer at the same time Liza heard her cell phone buzzing again. With a frown, she tried to ignore the sound, but it was odd anyone would be calling her so insistently when she was at work. *It certainly wouldn't be Tate*, she thought, and her friends and family knew her schedule. *Then who is it?* Distracted, Liza realized she had not heard the woman's answer. "I'm sorry. Could you repeat that?"

"Yes, it's Layton Clifton," the caller said.

"Thank you, Ms. Clifton," Liza replied as she typed her name into the computer database and started her record. Before she could continue, her phone chimed with not one text but multiple texts. *What is going on?* she wondered, feeling a little uneasy over someone being so insistent to talk to her. *I've got to check.* "Ms. Clifton, I apologize but I'll have to put you on hold for one second if that's all right?"

"Of course," the woman said, and Liza was thankful she had someone nice. Pulling her desk drawer open, she grabbed her purse and quickly pulled out her phone. On the screen were texts and missed calls from Rey. *That's weird*, she thought, her unease turning to worry. Rey would not be calling her unless there was a very good reason. Then her mind went to Tate and her situation at work. *Could this have something to do with that? But why would Rey be calling?* She had to know.

Turning to her coworker, Liza tried to stay calm. "Emma," she said. "Can you take the call that I have holding on line three? I have to check my messages. I think something serious has happened."

"I'm on it," her friend said, already reaching to press the number to answer.

"Thanks," Liza said as Emma started her conversation with Ms. Clifton. Stepping out of the office into the hallway, Liza quickly dialed Rey's number without bothering to read the texts or listen to the voicemail. "What's going on?"

"It's Nikki," Rey answered, and Liza heard tears in her friend's voice.

At the sound, Liza's heart nearly stopped. "What do you mean it's Nikki?" she asked. "Is she all right?"

"No," Rey's voice wavered. "A car hit her this morning while she was on her bicycle. The cops called me, because apparently, I'm listed as her emergency contact. I just got to the hospital."

"Oh my God," Liza said feeling her body go numb. *Not Nikki*, she thought. *That can't happen to Nikki. Nothing bad happens to Nikki.* "What hospital?"

"Good Samaritan," Rey said. "Can you come?"

"I'm calling Tate and then I will be on my way," she said. "It's going to be okay. Nikki is strong."

"I know," Rey said. "But she's in surgery, and they won't tell me anything else."

"I'll be there soon," Liza said hanging up to call Tate.

26

Trying to keep her composure as Aurora sat close beside her running her toes back and forth against Tate's shin, it was all she could do not to get up and walk away. Clearly the action was meant to be sensual, but Tate found the woman's actions repulsive. Unfortunately, without making a big, embarrassing scene there wasn't anything she could do about it. Even when she tried to move her leg away, Aurora shifted enough to keep at it. It was evident the woman took Tate's comments in the hall as a challenge and not a warning. *Because she knows there's nothing I can do about it*, Tate thought as she clenched her jaw. *The woman is untouchable right now. My boss thinks she's amazing and apparently, so do other executives if they gave her my promotion.* All of which only frustrated Tate more. Not only had Aurora received a high position at the firm, but she was abusing it to harass Tate. She had to try hard to focus on not losing track of what was happening in the meeting. Her part of the presentation was coming up soon and she looked forward to it. If nothing else but because it meant she could get away from Aurora's unwanted touching. When she was done talking, Tate planned to find another chair away from the woman. It might look odd, but at this point, she didn't care.

She felt her phone vibrate in her pocket. Reaching for it, she quickly silenced the buzz. Whoever was calling would have to wait. She was less than three minutes from her part. Unfortunately, the phone vibrated again. Clearly the person was insistent. *Maybe it's some sort of telemarketer call*, she thought. *Liza would never call me back-to-back. She knows how busy I am.* Again, she silenced the call and got ready to stand to make her way to the front of the room as her boss Chad was wrapping up the introduction. The phone vibrated a third time, making her pause. The insistent feeling of the calls made her wonder if something might be wrong. *But what? Is Liza okay? My family?*

After she silenced the thing again, a minute passed and Tate started to back up her chair, when an executive assistant knocked on the conference room door.

Chad frowned, but waved the assistant in. "What is it?" he asked when she poked her head in.

"I'm sorry to interrupt," she said. "But I have an urgent phone call for Tate."

"Urgent enough to interrupt this board meeting?" Chad asked with raised eyebrows.

The assistant paled. "Yes, the caller says so."

"I'll be right back," Tate said standing. Between the multiple calls to her cell phone and then the interruption by the assistant let her know…something was very wrong.

Chad frowned. "Wait a minute," he said. "Your section is up next. You can't leave."

Scanning the room, Tate pointed at her coworker near the front. "Maybe Walt can go next instead of me?" she asked. "It shouldn't impact anything."

Looking frustrated, Chad hesitated but then gave a sharp

nod. "Fine but his part is short so get back here. Don't make us wait on you."

Without another word, Tate rushed from the conference room taking her phone out of her pocket as she walked. As she suspected, the calls were all from Liza, but no voicemails. Clearly, her girlfriend wanted to talk to her directly, so she dialed Liza's number.

"Tate," Liza answered. "Thank God."

"Liza, what's wrong?"

"Everything," Liza said, and Tate could hear the woman was very upset.

Tate's mind raced as she thought of all the possibilities. If Liza wasn't the one who was hurt or in trouble, then maybe it was her parents. Or one of their close friends. Forcing herself to remain calm, Tate took a deep breath. "Tell me what's wrong," she said, and Liza paused as if trying to calm herself enough to speak.

"It's Nikki," she said in a quavering voice. "She's been in an accident. Apparently, somebody hit her while she was on her bicycle."

Feeling like she'd been punched in the chest, Tate stopped walking and for a minute had nothing to say. "Nikki?" she finally repeated back. "Is she... all right?

"No," Liza said. "I am on my way to the hospital to meet the others. How soon can you get there?"

Tate closed her eyes. She was in a horrible position. All she wanted to do was get to Nikki's side, but if she simply disappeared, Chad would be livid. She had to go back into the boardroom and give her part. It should only take fifteen minutes at the most. Then she would rush to the hospital.

· · ·

## TOGETHER AT RUBY'S

AFTER FINDING her way through the downtown streets of Portland to get to the hospital, Liza pulled into a parking spot and called Rey. "I'm here," she said. "Where are you?"

"We are all in the waiting area outside of post-op," Rey answered. "Nikki's out of surgery, but we still don't know anything."

"Okay," Liza said. "I'll be right there." In minutes, she found the waiting area and saw a concerned looking Marty standing near the entrance. Noticing Liza, her friend waved her over. Everyone was there except Tate. *But she's on her way,* she thought. *There's no way she wouldn't get here as quickly as she can. She and Nikki are so close.*

After hugging her friends, Liza sat beside Allie who had tears running down her cheeks. "What's happened?" Liza asked, with a sick feeling in her stomach while hoping things weren't worse.

"Nothing new," Rey said. "The only update is that she's out of surgery. The nurses won't tell me anything."

"That must count for something," Allie said in a shaky voice, and Liza's heart went out to her friend. Nikki was special to all of them, each in their own unique way, but Nikki was always Allie's protector.

Liza put her arm around Allie's shoulders and pulled her close. "Hey, this is Nikki we're talking about," Liza said. "She's invincible, right?"

"Right," Vivian said from where she sat on the other side of Allie holding her hand. "She'll pull through this. We need to be patient."

"Exactly," Marty added. "We will wait for the doctor and not jump to conclusions."

"Is that who we are waiting for?" Liza asked. "You mentioned that someone contacted you, Rey."

Rey nodded. "Yes," she said. "The police called, and that's how I found out that Nikki was in the hospital. Somehow, they got my number and called me at work to tell me Nikki Vander was in an accident."

Pausing for a moment, Liza absorbed what Rey said. Clearly Nikki had her as an emergency contact somewhere. "Did they tell you anything specific about what happened?"

"Not much," Rey said, shaking her head. "Only that the driver had run a stoplight and hit Nikki full force in the bike lane." Unable to help herself, Liza flinched at the image. She knew the damage had to be severe. *Thank God she's still alive*, she thought not letting herself think of the alternative.

"Was she wearing a helmet?" Liza asked.

"Yes," Rey said. "The policeman mentioned that and said it probably saved her life." No one said anything for a few minutes. Liza's mind raced through scenarios. She had seen hundreds of photographs of car crash damage. Crumbled metal, shattered glass. The idea Nikki, wearing only a helmet for protection, was hit by a moving car made her stomach ache.

Allie squeezed Liza's hand. "Is Tate on her way?"

"Yes," Liza said. "I contacted her through her assistant. She said she would come." Again, there was nothing but silence while they were all lost in their thoughts about what happened. Suddenly, it occurred to Liza she had no idea about Nikki's family. "Has anyone tried to contact Nikki's parents? They would certainly want to know about her accident."

The group all looked from one to the other. "I don't know anything about Nikki other than just what she's told all of us," Allie said. "I don't even know what kind of family she has."

"She must have parents," Liza said. "Maybe brothers and sisters. I mean we went to that fancy house for Christmas last year that was a friend of her father's."

"That's true," Vivian added. "But how we find them is the question."

Reluctantly returning to the boardroom, Tate stepped inside and realized no one was presenting. She walked to the front of the room. Apparently, Walt's update had been short and likely insignificant. *Just my luck*, Tate thought as she picked up the projector's remote and turned to look at the group. "Glad you could make it," Chad said with his voice full of sarcasm. "You're wasting all our time."

"I'm sorry, sir," Tate said. "Let me get started." Clicking to the first slide in her presentation, Tate looked at the screen for a moment and said nothing. The numbers. flowcharts, and graphs all seemed to run together. She gave that kind of information diligently over and over for the last ten years. It was who she was and what she did, and it made her good money. *But is that enough?* she wondered. *Do I want to do this for the rest of my life? Especially if I don't have leadership's respect?*

Chad leaned forward in his chair. "Are you going to say something?" he asked. "This is getting ridiculous." Tate looked at the man sitting in his business suit with an expensive tie. His hair was thinning on top and there were wrinkles on his face, but worst of all, he looked tired. He had aged a lot over the last ten years, but he was a lifer exactly like she thought she was. *Do I want that to be me?* she wondered. *Old and tired and still here giving presentations?*

Slowly she set the projector's remote on the boardroom's large table. "Actually, I won't waste any more of anyone's time here today." Tate scanned the room and saw the faces of her colleagues, all looked uncomfortable at what was transpiring. Some she had had drinks with, maybe even gone to some sort of promotional event with, but none were truly friends. *None are anything to me like Nikki*, she thought. "I'm going to go now." She turned to Chad. "My friend is in the hospital, and I need to be with her."

"You're not serious?" Chad said his face flushing with anger. "I think you need to reconsider what you're about to do. You're on thin ice already."

Tate's eyes widened. The words coming from a man she had respected and considered something of a mentor surprised her. Then she had a thought and looked down the table at Aurora Price. Unlike everyone else in the room, she was smiling, only to Tate it looked more like a smirk. In that instant she realized Aurora had been doing far worse than simply harassing her. She had talked to Chad behind her back clearly saying things that were not good for Tate's career. *She's trying to sabotage me,* Tate thought. *To keep me under her thumb.* It seemed crazy to Tate one person would do that to another, but she was not going to take the time to analyze it today. Combined with everything else that had been happening in Tate's life recently, it was too much.

She looked at Chad again. "Regardless," she said. "I am leaving right now." The man looked ready to say something, but Tate held up a hand. "If I'm not welcome back, then it is what it is. I'll be here tomorrow to discuss it." Without another word, she strode out of the boardroom and hurried toward the elevator. She had someplace to be, and it wasn't there.

## 27

Holding Allie's hand as they sat together on the uncomfortable vinyl couch, Liza forced herself not to tap her foot. Tate should be there, and she considered calling her again to find out what the delay was. Nikki was very important to Tate, and it made no sense she would let anything stop her from coming to the hospital. Just as Liza was about to take her phone out of her purse, she saw her girlfriend jogging down the corridor toward them.

Standing, Liza met her at the edge of the waiting area, and Tate enveloped her in a big hug. The feeling of the woman's strong arms around her, holding her tight, made everything a little less scary. Tate was strong on every level, and she was her rock. Finally letting go, Liza stepped back but kept her hand on Tate's arm as they moved further into the waiting area.

"Okay. Tell me the details," Tate said. "Everything we know." Her businesslike tone was exactly what everyone seemed to need to help them focus. Even Allie, who had not been able to stop her tears lifted her head to listen.

Her voice filled with emotion, Rey recounted everything

the group knew. Liza watched Tate's face as she absorbed the news. Only her eyes gave her away—fear for her friend.

When Rey was finished, Tate nodded. "Waiting on the doctor, it is," she confirmed and led Liza to another of the short couches.

"One other thing," Vivian added. "Do you happen to know how to reach Nikki's parents?"

Tate pursed her lips. "Actually, I don't," she said, surprising Liza. She was certain if anyone knew, it would be Tate. Apparently, Nikki was a closed book to all of them. "I don't know much about Nikki's background, but I think she has family somewhere back east. We never spoke about it in any depth." Tate sighed. "She's just Nikki."

Everyone nodded. "But we have to find out," Marty said. "We need to let them know. Someone."

"Did anyone try to see the contacts on her phone?" Vivian asked.

Rey nodded. "I looked but the phone is smashed and won't turn on."

"Wait," Tate said. "I do have a key to her condo."

Liza blinked. "You have a key?"

"Yes. She gave it to me a couple of years ago," Tate said. "When I asked her why, she grinned and said, 'just in case.'"

Feeling a little more optimistic, Liza rubbed Tate's leg. "Maybe there's something there that could tell us who to call," she said. "She has to have some sort of address list or something."

"But should we go look?" Rey asked. "I mean, she's super private."

Everyone was quiet for a few moments. "We won't look yet," Tate said. "Not until we hear from the doctor about how serious Nikki's prognosis is. Contacting them without something to tell them wouldn't be fair."

"When Nikki is awake, she could just tell us who to call,"

Liza added just as she saw a black man in scrubs coming their way.

By the way he walked with authority, Liza guessed he was the doctor. "I'm looking for Rey Madrona," the man said.

Rey stood. "I'm Rey."

"Good," the man said. "I am Dr. Saulsberry. I have an update about your friend, but I would really prefer to give the information to a family member." Liza watched everyone look from one to the other and she realized they might have a problem. Without someone from Nikki's unknown family, they would have to wait longer for information. It might even be impossible to find Nikki's parents, or someone related to her.

Taking control of the situation, Liza raised a hand. "I'm Nikki's sister, Liza," she said. "Please tell me how she is doing." The doctor paused, giving her face a once over. His reaction was not a surprise. Nikki was tall and blonde whereas Liza was small with dark hair and dark eyes.

The doctor nodded. "All right," he said finally. "Well, in that case I will let you know the good news is your sister was very lucky. She was wearing a bicycle helmet, and it saved her life. There's no serious head trauma." Liza felt like she could breathe for the first time since Rey's phone call earlier.

Unfortunately, the doctor wasn't finished. "The bad news is her body took the majority of the impact. She had internal bleeding that required surgery, and we removed her spleen. Also, her pelvis bone was broken as was her left leg and right arm."

"Poor Nikki," Liza heard Allie moan, but Liza gathered herself. There would be time to cry later.

"How is she now?" Liza asked, hoping they could see her.

"She's stable and medicated, so she will sleep. I suggest you go get some rest, and I can have a nurse notify you." The doctor paused, his face softening. "I can tell you right now,

Nikki's road back will be long and challenging. I am glad to see she has a large support network."

"Yes," Liza replied. "We all love her."

Arriving at Nikki's building, Tate and Liza walked through the lobby to the elevators. As they waited for it to arrive, Tate was filled with mixed emotions about invading her friend's privacy. As if reading her mind, Liza put a hand on Tate's shoulder. "Are you sure this is the right thing to do?" she asked, and Tate sighed.

"I don't like it," she said. "But I keep thinking about my parents. I know if I was in an accident as serious as Nikki's they would be desperate to find out." The elevator doors opened, and Tate led them aboard. "We need to see if there's any sign of family members to contact."

Apparently convinced, Liza nodded and when Tate opened the door to Nikki's apartment, they stepped into a small, but beautifully furnished room. The space looked like something out of a decorator's magazine, yet there was a feel of Nikki in the air. "Where do you want to begin? Liza asked, and Tate thought about it.

"I'd say her office if she has one, but from the few times I've been here, I don't remember her having anything but a bedroom." Glancing around the space her eyes landed on a small desk half hidden in the corner. "I guess with that." She pointed in its direction. "Maybe she'll have an address book or something."

Liza walked with Tate. "Something tells me our friend is not the type to have an address book laying around." Tate knew she was right. Everything about Nikki was modern and sophisticated, but they had to find something. Sitting on the tidy desk was a closed laptop. *If I was Nikki, any addresses I had would be on there,* Tate thought. *But there's no way it's not password protected.*

"Let's start with this," Tate said sitting in the black, leather desk chair. Opening the laptop, she powered it on only to be met with a password protection screen. *Just like I expected,* Tate thought. *And I have a sneaky suspicion it's a very complicated password.*

"What do you think that would be?" Liza asked, looking over Tate shoulder. "It's not like she has any pets."

Tate half smiled at her comment. "No, that is true," she replied. "And I doubt it's her birthday."

"What now?" Liza asked, and Tate reached for the first drawer on the desk, pulling it open.

"Maybe there's something here," she said but after a quick search of the desk they found nothing but the usual pads of paper, pens, and paper clips. No address book. *No pictures of anyone either,* Tate thought. *Not even an old Christmas card or something personal.* It felt off to Tate. Although she kept her desk organized, it was nothing compared to Nikki's.

Standing, she swept the condo with her eyes. Two tall bookcases stood on one wall and were filled with books. It was primarily nonfiction about a variety of topics. Everything from autobiographies, to philosophy, to true crime. There were a wide range of classics sprinkled in too. *How much do I really know about Nikki?* She wondered. *How much do any of us know her?* Nikki never hosted a game night or any of the other get-togethers, always claiming her space was too small. Frustrated, Tate wished she had taken the time to dig deeper and truly get to know her friend.

After a quick look through the simple, but efficient kitchen, opening some of the drawers hoping for some clue, they turned up nothing. There weren't even notes stuck under magnets on the refrigerator. That left only one place to try—Nikki's bedroom.

. . .

Although Liza had never imagined what Nikki's bedroom would look like, once she saw the room, it was a perfect fit. Decorated in black, grays, and chrome, everything about the bedroom said sleek, sexy, and capable. A king-sized bed sat in the middle flanked by nightstands. "I'll take that side," Liza said as she moved to the far side of the bed. A clock radio sat on the nightstand as well as a lamp, along with a pair of reading glasses and a thick paperback book. Picking it up, Liza read the title. "Atlas Shrugged" by Ayn Rand. *That's some deep bedtime reading*, she thought. *Not something I would envision Nikki picking. At least not the Nikki I thought I knew.*

Liza slowly pulled the top drawer open and froze. What she saw was the last thing she would've expected. Inside the drawer was what was clearly a handgun. "Tate," Liza said keeping her voice even. "Can you come look at this please?"

"What's wrong?" Tate asked as she quickly moved around the room to join Liza. "Oh wow."

"Oh, wow is right," Liza said. "Why does Nikki have a handgun? Beside her bed?"

"That is not something I can answer," Tate said softly, and Liza quickly closed the drawer.

"I don't want to search anymore," she said. "I think I may have crossed the line by seeing that gun. This is Nikki's private life."

Tate nodded. "You're right. We should go."

Thankful, Liza followed Tate through the condo, and they let themselves out. As Tate locked the door behind them, her phone chimed. Liza knew the sound by heart. It was a work email, which was not usually a good sign so late. Tate sighed. "What's wrong?" Liza asked. "Is that Aurora Price emailing you?"

"No, she wouldn't do anything like that," Tate said. "At

least not anything that would give her away. I have a feeling it's from Chad."

Liza raised an eyebrow. "Your boss Chad?" Liza asked as they walked toward the elevator. "Why do I get the feeling you think it will be bad?"

Pushing the elevator's call button, Tate winced. "Because I walked out in the middle of my presentation today. I told him I didn't want to waste anymore of anyone's time," Tate said. "He didn't take it very well."

"You did what?" Liza asked, a mixture of positive and negative emotions rolling through her as she thought of the consequences of doing something so drastic. "You should read the email."

As they stepped into the elevator Tate fished her phone from her pocket and read the message. She blew out her breath. "He wants me to come to his office first thing in the morning. I have a feeling that is not going to be a pleasant experience."

"How unpleasant?" Liza asked, her heart beating faster. "You don't think you're going to get fired over this do you?"

"Maybe," Tate said. "It's a combination of things actually. I think Aurora Price has been making up stuff and telling it to Chad. Things to make me look like incompetent."

Liza's face flushed. "I'm going to kill her," Liza said. "How could she do that to you?"

"She's trying to control me," Tate said. "And so far, she's getting away with it." Liza's mind whirled as she thought about what the ramifications would be if Tate got fired. A part of her was scared because it was the only life they knew, and the large salary made everything comfortable for them. Another part of her was exhilarated at the idea. Tate's job had encompassed their lives and taken Tate away from her evening after evening. So many weekends, especially over the last few years, were sucked up by Tate's job. She would not miss those parts when it was gone. *But if Tate doesn't work for that firm*, she thought. *What would she do? It's her whole identity.*

"You're awfully quiet," Tate said as they walked out of the building toward the car.

Liza took Tate's hand and pulled her to a stop. "Tate, I love you," she said. "And no matter what happens tomorrow, we will be okay."

## 28

Walking into the waiting room at the hospital, Tate saw Vivian with Allie cuddled up next to her on one of the small couches. It looked like Allie was asleep, and Tate hated to interrupt because her friend was taking the news extremely hard. Still, when Vivian saw them, she gave a little nod, and the movement was enough for Allie to open her eyes. Seeing them she sat upright. "Hey," she said. "Did you find anything?"

Tate shook her head. "Unfortunately, no."

"Well, that's not quite true," Liza added. "We did find something." Tate shot her a look but Liza either didn't register it or was determined to share what she had found. Tate had mixed feelings about telling the others about the gun in Nikki's nightstand. It was alarming of course to think their friend would need a weapon at her bedside but was also her private affair. *If there is a reason Nikki thinks she needs a gun*, Tate thought, *then is it for us to question it?*

"What did you find?" Vivian asked, and Liza sat on the couch across from them. "We found a gun," she said in almost a whisper. "In the nightstand beside her bed."

"What?" Allie said, her eyes wide. "Why would Nikki have a gun?"

"I know, right?" Liza said. "I mean, she's always been so mysterious, but I don't know what to think."

Tate held up her hands to slow them down. "Let's not jump to conclusions," she said. "Lots of people have weapons."

"Sure," Liza said looking at her. "But Nikki?"

Not wanting to talk about it anymore, Tate shrugged. "I'm just saying this is her business, and we need to pretend we never saw it."

"I agree with Tate," Vivian said. "We have other things to focus about right now."

Liza's eyes widened. "Why?" Liza asked. "Did you learn something new?"

Rubbing her red eyes, Allie took a deep breath. "No, nothing new," she added. "It's just all so horrible." A tear trickled down her cheek. Tate could understand how she felt. She was a mess inside over Nikki's situation, but it was never her style to let things show.

Hating to see how torn up Allie was, Tate reached a hand toward her. "Hey, want to go take a break?" Tate said when Allie took her hand. The woman clung on tight.

Vivian nodded. "That's a good idea," she said. "While you were gone, we decided to each take shifts in case Nikki wakes up unexpectedly. Allie and I are here until nine tonight and then Rey and Marty will take the night shift."

"They can't stay here all night," Tate said. "I'll come back at three a.m."

"Not without me," Liza said. "And I agree we can't let there be even the slightest possibility that Nikki wakes up and no one is here for her."

"That's what I was thinking too," Allie added.

Standing, Vivian helped Allie up. "We will go downstairs

and get a cup of coffee," she said. "Text us if anything changes."

"You know I will," Tate said. As the other two left, Tate sat beside Liza and put her arm around her shoulders to pull her closer. For a moment they sat in silence and then Tate felt Liza's body start to shake. Looking at her, she saw the woman's face had crumpled.

Tears started to flow, and she let out a sob. "We can't lose Nikki," she said. "She's a part of us. She's closer to me than family."

"I know," Tate replied, kissing her temple. "I feel the same. But she will pull through this. Keep believing in her."

Liza nodded and wiped her eyes. "But I can't stop thinking about what if it was you, Tate? I can't lose you."

The tears flowed harder. "You're never going to lose me," Tate said, and she felt her own heart ache at the thought of ever losing Liza. She never truly loved anyone unconditionally until she met her. It made her realize she wasted a lot of time. Working too many hours took her away from the woman she loved. *I am going to fix that*, Tate thought. *Somehow.*

Sitting in the waiting room waiting for Allie and Vivian to return, Liza held Tate's hand tightly. She rested her head on the woman's strong shoulder and could not sit close enough. What she said was true; she was more afraid than ever about losing Tate. Things had been crazy between them, and she almost made horrible mistakes. *But luckily*, she thought, *we found our way back to each other, and I'm never gonna let her go. Married or not, kids or not, it doesn't matter. All I want is to be with her.*

For a moment she thought about telling Tate what was in her heart, but then a young woman in light blue scrubs walked into the waiting area. Even under the sad circumstances, Liza noted the woman was very pretty. Strawberry blonde hair, friendly, but serious hazel eyes, and a warm smile that made Liza like her immediately. "Are you waiting for Nikki Vander?" she asked, and Liza nodded as she stood with Tate.

"We are," Tate answered. "Is there an update?" *It has to be good news,* Liza thought. *Or she wouldn't be smiling, right?* She felt her hopes rise.

The nurse shook her head. "Well actually, Nikki is already a challenging patient," she said with a little laugh.

Liza smiled. "That does not surprise me," she said. "Nikki is one-of-a-kind."

"I'm beginning to realize that," the young nurse said. "And even though she wasn't supposed to be awake already, she is.

"She's awake?" Tate asked and Liza squeezed her arm.

"Does that mean we can see her?"

"Yes," the nurse said. "For a brief amount of time, but she's asking for all of you. Particularly someone named Tate."

Liza heard her girlfriend let out a long breath of what was undoubtably relief. "I'm Tate," her partner said. "Can you take us to her?"

"Follow me," the nurse said and buzzed them through the door before leading them down a corridor of doors, some closed, some open and filled with patients. "She's right in here." The nurse pushed the ajar door open. "Nikki?"

When Liza looked, she had to stifle a gasp. The woman's face was pale under bruises and swelling. There was a large burn-like mark along one cheek that Liza guessed was from striking the pavement. *Thank God she was wearing a helmet,* Liza thought as Nikki opened her eyes. They were bloodshot and Nikki looked a little drugged, but Liza saw the essence of her friend in them and felt tears burn her eyes.

"Glad to see you," Nikki croaked, and Liza and Tate moved closer to the woman's bedside.

"Glad to see you more," Tate replied, her voice filled with emotion.

Liza took Nikki's hand. "I'm so glad you're awake," she said softly. "I was so afraid."

For a second it looked like Nikki might smile, but then she winced. "You know you should never worry about me."

The nurse cleared her throat at the end of the bed. "I'll leave you three alone for a few minutes," the young nurse said, and whisked out of the room.

Once she was gone, Nikki pointed at the door. "I'm going to marry that woman," she said, and Liza raised her eyebrows.

"Who? The nurse?"

"Yes," Nikki said. "When I opened my eyes, I was sure I was dead. She is who I saw, and I thought she was an angel."

Liza smiled. "I can see how that would affect a person," she said. "But still… are you sure it's not all the drugs you must be on?"

Again, Nikki tried to smile but with no luck. "Just you wait and see."

"Let's not talk crazy," Tate said. "You've always said you're not the marrying kind." Nikki looked at Tate, and Liza could almost read the communication flowing between them. She didn't know what it meant. but clearly Tate understood, and she gave a small nod. "But there's a first time for everything."

Liza watched Nikki's eyes struggling to stay open. "You can go to sleep, Nikki," she said. "We will arrange with the nurse to always have someone here with you."

"Wait, there's something I want to tell you before I fall back asleep," Nikki said. "It's why I woke up."

"What is it?" Liza asked, and Nikki's eyes continued to droop.

"You need to contact a woman named Danielle Salvador," she mumbled. For a second, Liza was confused, until she understood what the woman was trying to tell them and leaned closer as Nikki's voice weakened. "She's the reason Aurora Price left Chicago."

When Nikki made eye contact with Tate, her friend's subliminal message was not lost on her. In fact, it could not have been clearer if the woman shouted across the room. Nikki might have found someone new, but Tate had her own angel—Liza. Looking at her life, she had wasted enough time. Nothing would stop her from proposing when they got home. It would not be as romantic as she had envisioned, but tonight she needed Liza to know how much she loved her. *How much I want to spend the future with her,* she thought. *How much I want to have a family and grow old together.*

When Nikki followed with the name of someone who could help them with Aurora Price, Danielle Salvador, Tate was even more certain things were going to work out. If she could get ahold of the woman and talk to her about what was going on, it could make a huge difference. She felt confident getting Aurora out of their lives would allow things to go back to normal.

Wanting to thank Nikki for the information, Tate started to open her mouth when she realized Nikki's eyes were closed again. Her battered and broken friend was asleep. "I think we should go," Tate said to Liza, putting a hand on her lower back. "I will ask the nurse to let us know when she wakes up again. Let's go text the others."

Stepping out of the room, they walked to the nurse's station. The young nurse they first met stood with two others, and she turned when she heard them approaching.

"She's asleep again," Liza said. "We're going to go out into the waiting area and text her friends."

"That sounds perfect," the nurse said. "I'll check in on Nikki in a few minutes and make sure she's resting comfortably."

Tate nodded. "Thank you. I know she'll be in good hands. But how soon until we can start sitting with her?"

The nurse tapped her chin with her finger thoughtfully. "I'd say a couple of hours," she answered. "Believe it or not, she's still heavily sedated."

"Okay," Tate said. "Please keep us posted." She hesitated before walking away to the waiting area. "Nurse, what is your name?"

The nurse pointed to her badge clipped to her pocket displaying her smiling face above the name Lucy Madison. "I'm Lucy," the woman said. "And I understand you're Tate." She pointed at Liza. "But I didn't catch your name."

"And I'm Liza."

"Nice to meet you both. I imagine I'll be seeing quite a bit of you while Nikki is in my ward recovering."

With a smile, Tate put her arm around Liza. "Yes, you will," she said, then looked the young nurse in the eye. "Watch yourself with Nikki. She is… complicated."

"Is she now?" Lucy said with a tilt of her head. "Well, I feel confident I can handle the likes of her." Tate considered her words, and there was something about the woman's personality that made her think maybe Lucy was right.

29

In the kitchen, pouring her and Tate tall glasses of white wine, Liza could not believe how long the day had been. It seemed like days ago that she was hearing the bad news from Rey. Picking up the two glasses to join Tate in the living room, Liza could only hope that things would improve. "I'm so glad to be home," she said, holding out a glass to Tate. "I know we have to go back to the hospital later to relieve Rey and Marty, but it still feels good to be alone with you for a few minutes."

Nodding, Tate took the wine. "I agree," she said, and Liza noticed the woman's hand shaking.

"Are you all right?" Liza asked. "Why is your hand shaking?"

Tate hesitated as if unsure how to answer, and after a beat, she shrugged. "Just adrenaline, I guess. Left over from this evening and talking with Nikki," she said. "There's a lot to process."

Accepting the answer, Liza joined Tate on the couch. "It is a lot," she said. "I'm just glad that we got to talk to Nikki. She looks like hell, but this could have been so much worse."

"Yes. It could have been," Tate said sounding distracted.

Not sure what was wrong with Tate, Liza put a hand on her shoulder. "Seriously, Tate. What's in your head?"

"My head?"

"Yes," Liza answered. "You seemed very preoccupied with something. Is this over Nikki, or the news about finding someone to talk to about Aurora Price?"

Giving her a small smile, Tate covered her hand with her own. "All of that and more."

"I get it," Liza said. "What with the gun and that crazy business about Lucy Madison being an angel? It's all almost surreal."

After taking a sip of her wine, Tate nodded. "I never thought I'd hear the word marriage come out of Nikki's mouth. Our new friend Lucy doesn't know what she's got herself into."

"Or Nikki for that matter," Liza said, thinking about how confident the young woman seemed. It was clear she had dealt with many types of patients before and was not at all daunted by one more. *What she doesn't understand is Nikki will be difficult in a different way*, she thought. *When Lucy runs into Nikki's full charm, she might not know what hit her.*

Suddenly, Tate set her wine glass on the coffee table and turned to Liza. Her face was very serious. "I want to talk about us," Tate said abruptly. "When I was in the waiting room thinking about Nikki almost dying, I realized how short life can be." Surprised by the outburst, Liza didn't know what to say and Tate continued. "I can't lose you, Liza. I love you too much."

The words warmed Liza's heart. "I love you too," she said, thinking of how she felt in the waiting area too. "And I never want to lose you."

Tate stood. "I'll be right back." As Liza watched, the woman strode toward the bedroom. Surprised by her sudden exit, Liza hoped that Tate wasn't going to be sick. The distracted behavior was so unlike her. Before Liza could decide if she needed to go check on Tate, she returned, walking slowly toward her. "Liza. This is not how I envisioned everything going."

"What are you talking about?"

In answer, Tate took Liza's glass of wine and set it on the coffee table. "I expected to take you somewhere special and romantic," Tate continued. "But I listened to my heart, and this feels like the right time. And I don't want to wait to show you how much I love you."

For a second Liza was confused. She loved Tate's words, but she wasn't sure why the woman was giving them in what felt like a speech. Opening her mouth to ask what Tate was doing, she gasped when Tate dropped to one knee. Suddenly everything clicked. A fresh set of tears formed in her eyes, but these were for happiness.

"Liza," Tate held out a small, red velvet box. "I want you to be my wife." She opened the box and Liza saw the ring. The sparkle of the diamond offset by the rich red of the rubies was the most beautiful piece of jewelry she had ever seen. She covered her mouth with her hands and looked from the ring to Tate's face. Her girlfriend swallowed hard before continuing. "Will you marry me?"

When Liza didn't say anything at first, Tate thought the worst. Somehow, she had read all the signals wrong. She had waited too long to ask, and because of it, Liza was about to say no to her proposal. Unwilling to let that happen without at least trying to change the woman's mind, Tate opened her mouth to speak when Liza held up a finger. Slowly, she put it to Tate's lips.

"Don't say anything yet," she whispered. "I'm the one who

gets to talk now." All Tate did was take a breath. "I've been waiting for this day for so long. Sometimes it was all I could think about, and I resented you for not asking me." Tate watched as a tear ran down Liza's cheek. "And at last, you are on one knee asking me that magical question. But Tate…" Liza blinked back more tears. "I need to know. Are you sure this is what you really want?"

Surprised by the turn of events, Tate let her eyes drop from Liza's face. She stared at the ring, one she worked so hard to find. A ring that was as beautiful and unique as Liza. *Is this what I really want?* she wondered. *To be married and permanently responsible for someone else? Forever?* In an instant, she knew the answer and looked into Liza's waiting eyes again. "I'm sure," she said. "I want to be your wife as well as have you as mine."

"Oh Tate," Liza said somewhere between a sob and a laugh. "That's all I ever wanted."

"Then your answer is yes?"

"Yes, definitely yes."

Taking the ring from the box, Tate held it for Liza. "Then I think you should put this on," she said, and Liza put out her hand so Tate could slide the ring on her finger. It fit perfectly, just as Tate knew it would.

After holding the ring closer, Liza shook her head. "This is so beautiful," she said. "Where did you find it?"

"In a special shop downtown," Tate said. "It was quite a search, and that's where I was Friday. Finally, fate led me to just the right place and when I saw the ring, I knew." She sat on the couch beside Liza and took her hand. "Just like when I first saw you and I knew."

Liza's eyes misted with tears again and she took Tate's face in her hands. "And that's why you weren't at work?" she asked. "But didn't want to tell me?"

"Yes," Tate said. "I'm sorry it upset you so much."

With a sigh, Liza kissed her gently on the lips. "I forgive you."

Returning the kiss, Tate felt every ounce of Liza's love. And her passion. Filled with a fire that started from her core, Tate took the kiss deeper and was rewarded with a moan from Liza. Tate wanted her, wanted to celebrate being alive. Nikki's accident showed Tate all she took for granted, and she would work hard to appreciate each day going forward. Even though things at work were rough, she had an amazing life. She was happy and had the woman she loved with her. Slowly, she moved to take Liza in her arms and lift her to go to the bedroom, but Liza put a hand on her chest as she broke the kiss.

"Wait," Liza said. "Tonight, I want to be the one who pleases you."

GENTLY, Liza pushed Tate onto her back on the other end of the couch. At first Tate looked like she would resist, always the one to take control, but slowly she relented. Falling against the cushions without a word, Tate held Liza's eyes as she unhooked her belt, then unbuttoned her pants. When Tate sucked in a breath, Liza felt herself go wet at the prospect of taking control of someone as strong and as powerful as the woman before her. Pushing up Tate's shirt, Liza ran her lips over the woman's hard abs, feeling them quiver under her mouth. Then, without asking, she took hold of the waistband of Tate's slacks and underwear and pulled. Raising her hips to help, Tate growled when Liza smiled at the free access she had to Tate's center.

Once the pants and briefs were gone, Liza slid between Tate's legs and ran her tongue over the inside of her thigh. "Liza," she heard Tate say, starting to shift as if wanting to get up and turn the tables.

Liza slid her arms around Tate's toned thighs and held her in place. "Let me do this," she whispered. "Please." Relenting, Tate lay quiet but for the erratic sound of her breathing. "That's better." Continuing her teasing, Liza shifted to the other leg, tickling as she worked her way toward the middle. When she reached Tate's swollen folds, Liza ran a flat tongue over them.

In response, Tate bucked her hips and let out a moan. "You're killing me," she said. "I hope you know you will pay for it." The words made Liza even hotter. Tate was the perfect lover. Gentle when the mood called for it, more aggressive when Liza needed that instead. She looked forward to her punishment later. For the moment, it was all about Tate.

Running her tongue over Tate again, she went deeper, sliding between her lips to find her hard clit. "Is that better?" she murmured against Tate's burning skin and glancing up, saw Tate nod.

"Yes," she said. "More of that."

Happy to oblige, Liza licked again, circling Tate with her tongue. Once. Twice. She felt Tate's body tightening. The muscles in her thighs grew hard as she fought for control of herself. Tate was always the one in control. In the bedroom especially. *But not now,* Liza thought as she started to suck on her. *I'm the one in charge.*

Liza felt Tate's fingers run through her hair, taking hold of her in a gentle grip. The woman pulled Liza tighter against her and started to lift her hips in a rhythm to match Liza's sucking. Slowly, she added pressure as her hips moved faster. "That's it," Tate said from deep in her throat. "That's it." Knowing her lover was close to the edge, Liza used all her mouth. She pulled and licked until the heat at Tate's core started to melt. "That's it." The words were more of a roar than before, and Liza knew she had her. In a burst of shaking, Tate started to throb under Liza's tongue as the orgasm rocked her. Every part of Tate seemed to let go until after a moment, her movements slowed. Tate's hand slipped away from Liza's hair, and she heard the woman let out several deep breaths. "That was fantastic."

Liza smiled as she licked her lips. "Thank you," she said. "Now, take me to the bedroom."

## 30

At the hospital, while they took shifts sitting with Nikki, Tate took time to do a little research on her phone. As she sat with Liza on the bench seat near the window and Nikki slept, she searched for Danielle Salvador. There were, unfortunately, quite a few of them in Chicago. *I'm going to have find a way to narrow this down*, she thought. *I should have known it wouldn't be so easy.* "Why don't you try searching for where Aurora Price worked?" Liza suggested in a whisper as she looked over Tate's shoulder. "That must be their connection."

Liking the idea, Tate nodded and typed in 'Aurora Price Chicago'. Google brought back several hits for her. Tate had to admit, Aurora had quite the résumé. On paper she looked like an amazing person, and Tate had trouble reconciling the two personalities. There were articles about her winning awards for her volunteer work with children who had Multiple Sclerosis. She was also a standout with one of Chicago's biggest investment firms. When Tate clicked on a link that took her to yet another stellar article, she saw the face of the beautiful woman who was harassing her. *She really is attractive*, Tate thought. *It doesn't make sense why she takes advantage of her power to make people do things against their will. But maybe that's what it really is—all about power.*

As if reading her mind, Liza pointed at the picture on Tate's phone. "Why would someone so beautiful, who seems to have everything, be so horrible?" Liza asked quietly.

"I'm not sure," Tate replied in a murmur. "I was just thinking she does it to feel powerful."

"Crazy, but now we know where she worked," Liza said. "Maybe check out their website and see if you can find Danielle."

After a few tries, Tate found an obscure connection between Danielle Salvador and the firm where Aurora used to work. She had been an intern there. Unfortunately, there was no contact information for her. *So, what do I try next?* she wondered and then had an idea. Quickly she typed in Danielle Salvador's name again, searching for where she was an alumnus. Immediately her name came up with University of Chicago. "I wonder if I can contact their alumni office?" Tate said to Liza.

"That sounds like a good idea to me," Nikki said from her bed. "You've got to track her down."

"Hey," Liza said standing to go to Nicky's bedside. "We didn't mean to wake you."

"It's all right," Nikki said. "I could use a drink of water." Tate watched as Liza used the plastic glass beside Nicky's bed to give her a sip of water through a straw. She was tender and gentle, and in that instant Tate realized she would be a great mom. There was a nurturing side to her that wasn't always evident until situations like helping Nikki. It made Tate love her all that much more. *I'm glad she's going to be my wife*, she thought. *And the woman I raise kids with.*

Watching them, Tate was curious. "Nikki, how did you find out about Danielle and Aurora having a connection?"

Nikki sipped more water, before shrugging her good shoulder. "I just know a guy who knows a guy who is in Chicago." Liza and Tate made eye contact at Nikki's vague answer. Tate hesitated to dig deeper. *Not today,* she thought. *But maybe one of these days, when she's better...*

Tate stood and kissed Liza on the cheek. "I'll make a call to the university once they open in a few hours," Tate said. "But first I need to go home and take a shower. I just hope I have time to get ahold of Danielle before I have to face the music with Chad.

"Are you sure there's no one you want us to reach out to?" Liza asked. "To at least let them know you're in the hospital?"

Nikki started to shake her head but then winced. "I'll take care of all that later," she said. "There's no one who needs to know I'm in the hospital." From the tone in Nikki's voice, Liza knew the conversation was pretty much over. It made no sense to her there wasn't anyone in Nikki's life who would think her being injured warranted attention. Yet it seemed to be the case, and Liza would not press it further. *She's so complex*, Liza thought, and her mind returned to finding the gun in Nikki's bedside table. *There's a story here, but I wonder if we'll ever learn i*t.

There was a quiet knock at the door and in walked Lucy. "How are we doing in here?" she asked. "It's nice to see you awake, Nikki."

Nikki tried to smile but again winced. "It's even nicer to see you."

Lucy shook her pretty head. "You're just saying that because I am the one who gives you the good drugs."

"Well... that is part of it I'm sure," Nikki said. "But you're different than all the other nurses. Seeing you makes me feel better."

"Well, thank you," Lucy said. "But they're all very competent, and I'm here to let you know my shift is over. I'm going to head out for the day."

Liza watched Nikki's face fall. "Okay," she said disappointment clear voice. "When are you back?"

"I'll be back in twelve hours," Lucy said after checking Nikki's vitals and logging them in the room's computer.

There was another knock at the door. "Come in," Nikki said, and Allie walked in to join them.

"Oh good," she said. "You are awake."

"So it seems," Nikki said with some of the old familiar playfulness in her voice. "Thank you for coming, Allie."

Lucy gave them all a little wave. "Bye for now," she said as she left the room. "Be good, Nikki."

Liza watched her go. "She's nice."

"I like her too," Allie said.

Knowing Nikki had feelings for Lucy, Liza gave her a look. "You seem fond of her too."

"I'm more than fond of her," Nikki said. "I'm going to marry her."

Liza glanced at Allie whose eyes were wide. "What did you say?" she asked, making Liza laugh.

"Yes, Nikki's said that a couple of times now," Liza said. "But I'm still not convinced it's not the drugs talking."

"True, the drugs are great," Nikki said. "But mark my word. Lucy Madison will someday be my wife." Liza smiled, wondering if it could be true. *Can Lucy be the one who tames our Nikki?* she wondered. *Maybe.*

KNOWING she couldn't put it off any longer, Tate made her way toward her boss's office. She had made a call to the woman she hoped was the correct Danielle Salvador and left a rather direct message. She needed information on Aurora

Price as soon as possible. Tate worried Danielle would ignore it. If Tate received a call from a stranger asking for information, she might not return it. Hopefully, this wouldn't be the case.

Reaching Chad's office, she stopped in front of his assistant's desk. The young man didn't look away from his computer terminal, leaving Tate standing there almost a full minute before Tate cleared her throat. "I'm here to see Chad," she said. "He wanted to see me first thing this morning."

The executive assistant finally looked at Tate, and she didn't like the dismissiveness in his eyes. "Hold on, I'll tell him you're here." Picking up the desk phone's receiver, the assistant pressed a button. "Ms. Nilsen is waiting for you." Tate raised an eyebrow. *Now I'm Ms. Nilsen?* she thought. *This is getting worse by the second.* The assistant hung up. "He'll come get you in a minute." Not appreciating the fact that she was getting the cold shoulder, all Tate did was nod. It was part of the power game that she never knew Chad would play, and she was disappointed. Even as she worked her way up the ladder at the firm, she had never tried to make anyone feel inferior. Today it felt like that was exactly what her boss was doing.

Finally, after Tate checked her watch and saw more than ten minutes had passed, the door to Chad's office opened, and he waved for her to come in. "I'm ready for you," he said, his voice empty of any friendliness. With a sigh, Tate followed him into his office and waited while he sat behind his desk. Tate didn't bother to take a chair, feeling the conversation would be short.

The man looked at her, and she saw nothing but irritation in his eyes. "Tate," he said. "I don't have time for this crap, so let's get to the point."

"All right, sir," Tate said with a nod.

Chad glared at her. "You have been underperforming."

The words hit Tate like a slap in the face. After a decade of hard work for the firm with multiple performance reviews in which she always had stellar marks, to be told she was underperforming seemed unfair.

"I—," Tate started when Chad held up a hand.

"I don't need input here," he said. "Basically, it looks like you're cutting corners when serving our clients."

"Cutting corners?" Tate spat, so surprised that she couldn't keep her mouth shut. "I don't even know what you're talking about."

"Well, let's take your attitude yesterday," he said. "Clearly, you're no longer focused on your work. Nobody walks out of a meeting in the middle of their presentation and keeps their job for much longer." The threat hung in the air. "The only reason you're still here is Aurora Price said she'd keep mentoring you. It's clear you still have a lot to learn."

Shocked by one incredible statement after another, Tate found herself trying to figure out what to say. *Should I tell him about Aurora Price harassing me?* she wondered. *Or would he only think I am grasping at straws to explain my behavior. And have I been cutting corners?* Tate didn't think so, but suddenly she questioned everything. It could be the reason why he didn't give her the promotion. *But why wouldn't he talk to me first?*

"Do you have anything to say for yourself?" Chad asked, and Tate had the strongest desire to tell him that she quit, but swallowed hard and shook her head.

"No, sir," she said. "Other than I promise to do better."

"We'll see," Chad said. "You can go."

Walking out of the office, Tate held her head high as she passed the executive assistant's desk. She felt his eyes boring into her back and knew without a doubt he was passing judgment on her. *Aurora is turning this entire firm against me,* she thought. *How can this be happening?*

Before she made it back to her office, her cell phone rang, and she fished it out hoping the call was from Danielle Salvador. The number was not the same she had dialed previously, and for a second she thought about letting it go to voicemail, but her instinct told her to answer it. "This is Tate," she said.

There was a long pause, and she thought for a second the person had hung up but then there was a sigh. "Hi," the voice said. "This is Danielle Salvador. I understand you want to talk to me about Aurora Price."

"Yes," Tate said with excitement as she entered her office and shut the door. "I'm having an issue with the woman here where I work, and your name was given to me as someone I should contact."

"What do you want to know?"

Tate didn't even know where to begin. "Anything you can tell me. Frankly, she's making my life hell."

"Uh-huh," the woman said through the phone. "That sounds like Aurora. Well, good luck."

Tate frowned. "Good luck?"

"Yeah," Danielle said, her voice turning hard. "She's poison. I want to know who gave you my name."

Tate hesitated, not wanting to cause trouble for Nikki, but not wanting Danielle to hang up either. "A friend of mine is looking into Aurora's background. Your name came up."

"Great," Danielle said. "Well, I will say this. If she's bothering you, then you're in trouble—that woman ruined my entire career before it even got started."

## 31

As she finished getting ready for work, Liza's phone rang. *It's either Tate or about Nikki,* she thought, feeling uneasy. She and Tate would go back to the hospital later that evening to sit with Nikki, so she hoped that wasn't it. But if it was Tate, it couldn't be a good sign if she was calling from work already. *Things must not have gone well with Chad,* she thought. *I hope she's okay.* "Hello," Liza said as she answered the phone.

"Hey," Tate said, sounding frustrated.

Liza frowned. "How did it go?"

"Ugly," Tate said. "I think Aurora Price has been doing more damage than I realized. He said I was underachieving and cutting corners."

"He said what?" Liza said, her temper rising.

Tate sighed through the phone. "Yes, according to him, I still have a lot to learn." Stunned by her girlfriend's words, Liza did not know what to say. She was so angry she was ready to smack something. *I am going to tear that woman's hair out,* she thought. *She can't do this to Tate. She's worked too hard and for too long to be torn down now.* Before she could come up with a comment, Tate continued. "But that's not why I'm calling. I heard back from Danielle Salvador."

"Oh," Liza said. "I need the details of that."

"Yes, it was an interesting conversation, and I feel bad for her," Tate said. "Aurora Price really did a number on her."

"Like what?" Liza asked.

"Danielle told me she was an intern at the firm in Chicago where Aurora worked. After only two weeks, Aurora started coming on to her much like she's coming on to me.

"With an intern?" Lies asked. "That's even more disgusting."

"Yes, I agree," Tate said. "But Aurora clearly likes playing with people. Unfortunately, it got so bad the intern felt she had to sleep with her in order to keep her job."

"Oh God," Liza said.

"It gets worse," Tate said. "Although Danielle wisely hid a video camera to capture their interlude, it backfired on her."

Liza tried to imagine what could possibly have gone wrong. "Even that wasn't enough proof?"

"Not exactly," Tate said. "Apparently, the outcome was that the firm asked Aurora to leave quietly but not because she was sexually harassing Daniel Salvador."

With a shake of her head, Liza guessed the reason, and it made her even angrier. "Because she had slept with an intern," she said. "Which did nothing to stop the actual problem."

"Right," Tate said. "She just found a new firm in a new city and started up again. Only we don't have any interns right now."

"And now she is targeting you," Liza stated. "What do we do now? Take this back to Chad?"

"I don't think he'd listen to me at the moment," Tate answered. "But the videotaping got me back to thinking about how we want to record a conversation with her. I need to confront her and make her say something that will incriminate her."

"You said that would be almost impossible at work," Liza replied. "Why would it work now?"

Hearing her girlfriend let out a deep breath, Liza knew she was beyond frustrated. "I don't. So, what do you think I should do?" Tate asked. "Take her somewhere public? I don't think she'll say anything stupid with people around."

"Unless you took her out somewhere you had a little privacy... like a bar," Liza said as an idea formed in her head. "Tate, ask Aurora out for a drink after work tonight."

"A drink?" Tate asked sounding confused. "Isn't that sending the worst message?"

"It will be okay," Liza said. "Just bring Aurora Price to Ruby's."


AFTER PARKING her car in the small lot behind the bar, Tate waited for Aurora to catch up with her. The woman was absolutely beaming with satisfaction. Plastering a smile on her face, Tate led the way around the corner of the building toward Ruby's front door. As they walked Aurora slipped her arm through Tate's as if they were on a real date. Tate stiffened but did not dare to pull away. Aurora couldn't have any clues to what Tate was planning. "This place you are taking me to," Aurora purred. "Do you come here often?"

Tate shrugged. "Once in a while," she said. "It's one of the hangouts in Portland that is LGBTQ+ friendly."

"Perfect," Aurora said as they neared the door. "I can't tell you how excited I was when you asked me out for a drink tonight. I'm glad you are starting to..." She hesitated for a beat. "...understand our relationship." Tate didn't comment as she opened the door and let the woman walk through. Ruby's was half full of mostly familiar faces. Vivian was behind the bar while Allie and Marty were on stools across from her. Tate glanced at them, but the plan was to pretend she didn't know anyone very well.

As she looked, Vivian gave a subtle nod in the direction of the horseshoe booth. "Let's sit over here," Tate said leading Aurora. Tate had no idea what the exact plan was but clearly something was in the works. She simply had to run with it and hope everything worked out. Sliding into the booth, Tate was surprised when Aurora moved to sit next to her rather than across the table. Uncomfortable, Tate went all the way to the middle of the horseshoe. Aurora followed. Even though there was space for eight or more people, they were almost shoulder to shoulder. *All part of the game,* she thought. *I just need to get her talking.*

Aurora picked up the drink menu already on the table. "What shall we have?" Aurora asked, giving Tate a knowing look. "I mean in a drink." She winked. "I love a good cocktail, so I hope the bartender knows what she's doing."

Tate swallowed hard. "I'm more of a beer person."

"How sexy of you," Aurora said with a little laugh. "You really are something, Tate."

Deciding there was no better time to act, Tate forcefully moved away from Aurora and looked her in the eye. "Actually, I brought you here because I wanted to have a private conversation." Aurora looked surprised at her sudden movement but said nothing. "I don't like the way you're treating me at work. It's harassment."

"Oh Tate," Aurora said with a shake of her head. "I think you are lying. You know you love it." She reached across the table to rest a hand on Tate's forearm. "But I appreciate that you're playing hard to get. We both know there is incredible chemistry between us." She gave Tate a sultry stare. "There's nothing wrong with acting on it."

"There is to me," Tate said. "I've asked you more than

once to stop coming on to me, but you're not listening." She looked hard into Aurora's eyes. "In fact, I've made a few inquiries in Chicago."

Aurora's eyes narrowed. "You did what?"

"I contacted someone to find out if you did something like this before," Tate answered. "You know, harassed someone at work."

"Oh, you've got to be kidding me," Aurora said, rolling her eyes. "And what lies did you uncover about me?"

"Well, I learned you had to leave Chicago because of an incident with a young woman in the workplace."

Aurora's face grew angry. "I don't like how this conversation is going," she said. "If you talked to that Salvador woman, she is spinning a tale about something you don't know anything about." A sinister smile crossed her face. "I suggest that you rethink your actions here tonight."

"Or what?" Tate asked, feeling her own temper rising. She did not like to be threatened. "What will happen to me if I continue to say no to you?"

Aurora laughed. "I don't think you want the answer to that," she said. "But let me guess, you were thinking of going to Chad with what you uncovered, weren't you?"

"That's exactly my intention," Tate said.

Aurora rolled her eyes. "You're being ridiculous," Aurora said. "It would be your word against mine, and frankly, your position with the firm isn't exactly solid right now. Let's face it. You would lose."

Sitting in her car across the street from Ruby's front door, Liza had waited until she saw Tate and Aurora Price coming toward the bar. It was hard not to react when she watched Aurora slip her arm through Tate's and cuddle in closer. *That woman is going to be so sorry she messed with us*, she thought.

*She really deserves this.* Dialing Allie's phone number, her friend answered on the first ring. "They are coming in," Liza said. "Get ready."

After Liza explained to her friends about the situation with Aurora Price, and asked them to help set her up, they were more than willing. They loved Tate too. The plan was simple. Allie was going to leave the call open and put the phone in the potted plant behind the horseshoe-shaped booth. Liza would be able to hear everything Tate and Aurora said and record it using Marty's phone. All Tate had to do was make Aurora say something incriminating.

Listening, Liza heard them slide into the booth, Aurora flirting, and then Tate telling Aurora to stop. When Aurora laughed, Liza was about ready to storm into the building, but she needed the woman to say a little bit more. Aurora gave it to her. "It would be your word against mine and frankly your position with the firm isn't exactly solid right now. Let's face it. You would lose."

After a fist pump, Liza turned off the recording and hung up the phone. With her own smirk of satisfaction, she marched into Ruby's and strode to the booth where Aurora and Tate sat. Aurora looked at her, surprise in her eyes. She glanced from Liza to Tate and back. "Wait," she said. "Aren't you the girlfriend?"

"Actually, I'm not," Liza said putting a hand on her hip. "I am the fiancée."

Aurora looked at Tate. "Did you know she was going to be here?"

"Yes, actually I did," Tate said with a small smile. "I lied about coming to Ruby's. I come here multiple times a week, and I consider this place my second home."

Just then Liza felt Allie and Marty and Vivian come up beside her. "It's all of our second home," Allie said. "And we're all like family."

Liza saw Marty cross her arms. "And we don't like it when someone tries to hurt one of our own."

"That's all quite charming," Aurora Price said with a smirk. "Are you going to take me out back and beat me up like some gang?"

"No," Liza said. "We don't have to do that." She held up Marty's phone. "We have more than enough of your conversation to do better."

Aurora narrowed her eyes. "What are you talking about?" she asked. Liza handed Marty the phone, and Marty quickly pulled up the voice app to push play. Aurora and Tate's voices were crystal clear and so was the fact Tate was being harassed against her will. "I am going to go now." Aurora slipped from the booth, pushing past Liza and her line of friends.

"Yeah, you do that," Liza said. "Get out, and not just out of Ruby's, but out of Portland altogether."

## 32

Tate marched up to Chad's executive assistant's desk and saw her boss's door was closed. Considering it was early in the morning, he might be still out, yet his assistant was there. Historically, he started when Chad started, which let Tate know the man was in his office. "I need to see Chad," she said firmly. "Immediately."

The assistant gave her a cold look. "He's in a meeting," he said. "You'll need to set up something on his calendar."

Putting her hands on his desk, Tate leaned in to speak directly into the assistant's face. "I'm going to see him now," she said finally sick of the runaround and getting attitude from someone who was beneath her on the org chart. "Please let him know I'm coming in. Now."

"Wait a minute," the assistant said, and his face flushed. "You can't just barge in—"

"That's exactly what I intend to do," Tate said and without another word opened the door and walked into Chad's office. The man looked from his desk surprised but not as surprised as Tate was to see the auburn-haired woman sitting in a chair in front of his desk. Aurora Price was the one Chad was meeting with and she felt her stomach clench. *This cannot be good for me*, she thought. *She knew what I would be doing first thing this morning.*

Chad leaned back in his chair. "That was some entrance," Chad said. "You didn't even bother to knock?"

Tate walked toward him. "This is important," she said not bothering to apologize. "Something that can't wait."

"What good timing," Aurora said with the lift of her chin. "We were just talking about you."

"I'm sure you were," Tate said, unable to keep the contempt out of her voice. "Just like I'm sure you're putting a spin on what happened." She reached into her pants pocket and held up a small recording device. "But proof is proof."

Chad shook his head. "I'm not so sure I believe in your proof," he said. "From what it sounds like, you manipulated her and led her on. Entirely inappropriate."

"That is not what happened," Tate said, her hand clenched into a fist. "She has been sexually harassing me since the first day she started at the firm."

"And you're going to tell me this has nothing to do with her getting your promotion?" Chad asked with a sneer. Finally, the truth was out there. The man had admitted Aurora Price had gotten what should've been Tate's promotion.

She lifted her chin. "Is that what happened?" she asked. "You gave it to her for some reason after all but promising it to me?"

"Nothing was promised you," Chad snapped. "And Aurora and I go back a long way. We went to college together."

Suddenly the pieces of the puzzle fell into place for Tate. Chad had known Aurora from the past. That was the reason she was able to make the move from Chicago so seamlessly. Clearly, Aurora called in a favor when she was in a pinch.

"Regardless," Tate said. "I'm taking my evidence to HR

and letting them know what has been happening here at the firm."

Aurora sat up in her chair. "You wouldn't dare."

With a wry smile, Tate put the recorder in her pocket. "Oh, I definitely dare," she said. "I only came in to tell Chad in advance to give him warning."

"You're making a mistake," Chad added. "If you go to HR with that, nothing good will come of it."

Starting to back up, Tate had heard enough. "Really?" she asked. "That almost sounds like a threat."

"It's not a threat," Chad said. "It is a promise. This is your last warning. It appears you have been incompetent for a long time. Somehow hiding it from all of us."

The word incompetent made Tate feel sick. She knew in an instant she was burning bridges that would be hard to recover from. But one thing was clear, her time at the firm working with Chad was over.

"In that case," Tate said. "After my trip to HR, I won't be coming back. I quit."

While keeping Nikki company, Liza's phone buzzed. When she looked at it, there was a text from Tate. "Where are you?" was all it said.

She quickly wrote back that she was at the hospital until noon, and then she would be going to work. "How did it go with Chad?"

"I'll tell you in a minute," Tate wrote back.

Not sure what Tate meant, Liza looked at Nikki. "Well, I don't think her conversation with Chad went very well," she said. "The text she just sent is confusing."

Nikki winced. "That's not what we want to hear," she replied. "The situation with Aurora Price needs to stop."

"It does," Liza agreed. "It's really weighing on her, I can

tell. She tries to hide it from me, but I can see the unhappiness in her eyes."

There was a sharp knock on the door. "Come in," Nikki said, and Liza was surprised to see Tate. There was a smile on her face that Liza took to be a good sign. However, the fact that she was at the hospital and not at work confused her. *She should be in her office working with clients if everything is okay*, she thought. *There's a reason why she's here and not there.*

"Hi," Nikki said.

Striding in, she stepped up to Liza. "Good morning," she replied and pulled Liza into her arms before giving her a kiss on the lips.

"What's that for?" she asked when Tate pulled back. "And seriously, why are you here? Shouldn't you be at work?"

Tate shook her head. "About that," she said. "I'm actually done for the day." Liza searched her face and noticed the stress she told Nikki about seemed to have dissipated. It looked like Tate was relaxed. She was happy.

"Okay," Liza said. "Do you want me to take the rest of my day off? I'd rather not because I've missed so much work, but…"

Slipping her arm around Liza's waist, Tate smiled. "Not necessary," she replied. "I'll just hang here with Nikki today."

"I like the sound of that," Nikki said. "Maybe I can convince you to sneak out and get me a beer and a pizza."

Tate laughed. "I'm sure things could be arranged," she said was a wink.

Liza narrowed her eyes. Tate was acting weird but in a good way, and she wanted to get to the bottom of it before she left. "Tate, I think I need a little more information," Liza said. "Like how it went with Chad this morning?"

"Awful," Tate said, with a chuckle. "It could not have gone worse."

Completely confused, Liza furrowed her brow. "Then why are you in such a good mood?"

"Because," Tate answered with a shrug, "I finally did what I should've done a long time ago."

Liza felt her chest tighten with anxiety as she contemplated what Tate meant. "And that is?"

"Yeah," Nikki said. "Don't leave us in suspense. Tell us the good news."

Tate beamed. "I finally quit."

Scared half to death, but unable to stop smiling, Tate watched Liza's face. Several emotions seemed to flash through her eyes as she processed what Tate told her. The news was massive and would change both their lives significantly. *It's probably something I should've talked over with her first,* Tate thought. *But at the moment, I just acted. No matter how much it might make things difficult for us for a while, I know it was the right decision.* Suddenly, Liza gave Tate a hug, and it felt amazing to be in her woman's arms. She held her tight, and they stood for a minute, holding each other.

When Liza pulled back, there were tears in her eyes, but Tate couldn't tell what they were from. "Babe, you're crying," Tate said. "Does this upset you that much?"

Liza wiped her eyes and smiled. "No, well, yes, but no. It's just so sudden," Liza said. "But I believe you when you say it's the right decision, and so I support you."

"It was what I had to do," Tate said, and it was true. The more she thought about it, the more certain she became that quitting was her only option. "I realize this is scary, but I also know we are strong if we stick together. Everything will turn out all right."

Liza touched Tate's face and nodded. "That is the truth."

"I think it's great news," Nikki said. "You're too good for that place anyway."

Take chuckled. "I think you may be right."

"So, what happened with Chad that you quit your job?" Liza asked. "Was it that bad?"

"It was," Tate replied. "When I barged into his office, I was shocked to see Aurora Price was already there. Covering her ass."

"That woman is incredible," Liza growled. "Evil."

"But she's smart," Tate added. "She had already started spinning her web of lies with Chad before I even got there."

"He believed her?" Liza asked. "Even though you had proof?"

Thinking of how it all happened, Tate shook her head. "I never got a chance to play it for him," she said, feeling angry all over again. "It turns out that he and Aurora went to college together. That's how she got the job so easily at the firm."

"That explains a lot," Nikki inserted. "I knew there had to be something for you to not get that promotion."

Smiling again, Tate pointed at Nikki. "But maybe it is for the best," she said. "Maybe it's just what I needed to make a change."

"So, what are you going to do now?" Liza asked. "Other than take the time off that you deserve."

Her question was a good one. "I guess I'll refresh my résumé and start making some phone calls," Tate answered. "Chad will probably spread some rumors about me and make it harder for me to find another position as high up as I was there." She looked into Liza's eyes. "I might have to start back at the bottom. I'm sorry."

Before Liza could respond, Nikki held up her good hand to get their attention. "That's the last thing you should be doing," she said. "What you should be doing is investing some capital with me and buying the gym."

Tate felt a sliver of excitement at the idea of following her heart and owning the gym, but it was ridiculous to think she could do it. "I don't know the first thing about running a gym," Tate said. "I like your faith in me, but we have to be realistic."

Liza touched Tate's face, taking back her attention. "You are the smartest person I have ever met," Liza said. "I know you could make any business a success. If you really want this, I will stand beside you." She kissed her. "I just want you to be happy."

For the second time that day, Tate decided to jump off the edge into the abyss of uncertainty. "Then let's do it," she said. "Let's buy the gym."

## 33

"You look so beautiful," Allie said as Liza turned her body left and then right while looking in the full-length mirror.

She had to agree. The dress fit her like a glove and after all their searching, it seemed perfect. "I do like it," she said. "And more importantly, I think Tate will like it."

"How could she not?" Rey added from where she sat watching Liza on the bench seat in the bridal gallery's dressing area. "You'll take her breath away in that."

Overall, that was what Liza wanted the most—to be a beautiful bride. Not only because it was a dream she had since she was a little girl, but because Tate deserved it. "Then this is the one," Liza said. "I can put it on payments for the next couple of months." She laughed, and it was filled with excitement but also nervousness. "I can't believe the wedding is only three months away. There's so much to do."

Standing from where she sat beside Rey, Allie took Liza's hands and kissed her on the cheek. "It's been a long time in the making but will be perfect," she said. "I'm so happy for you both."

"Thank you," Liza said. "And thank you and Rey for being a part of it."

Rey stood and joined them until all three friends were reflected in the large mirrors. "Wouldn't miss it for the world," she said. "And the reception you're planning too. It will be wonderful." Liza had to agree. The decision to hold it at Ruby's was an easy one. The place was as important to her as any person she invited. It was where she and Tate met, where they had so many memorable nights, and where they had foiled Aurora Price. There was nowhere she would rather celebrate her marriage to Tate.

Remembering they had someplace to be soon, Liza glanced around for her phone. "What time is it?" she asked, and Rey quickly checked her watch.

"Only four o'clock," she answered. "We are fine on time. I've been keeping track."

Liza smiled at her friend. "Perfect," she said. "But help me get this dress off so I can go make arrangements. I definitely don't want to be late for Tate's grand reopening."

"That is so exciting, too," Allie said, unlacing the back of Liza's dress. "I know Tate and Nikki will make it a huge success."

Liza beamed with pride. "I agree with you," she said. "Between them, they've made great plans and already implemented some. I think the regulars will love it, and the facelift will draw new clientele as well." She looked over her shoulder at Allie. "Your design of the new logo and other suggestions around marketing were a big help too."

"It was the least I could do," Allie said. "Especially since I've never seen Tate look happier."

Rey nodded. "She certainly seems to be," she said. "I've never seen her talk so much about any topic. It's great to see."

"It's true," Liza said, stepping out of the dress. "Leaving

the firm and buying the gym was the best thing that ever happened to her. I wish it happened earlier."

"But you had no idea it would be this good," Allie added, and Liza knew it was true. Her time with Tate was better and better every day. Even though she had been scared at first, the change was clearly the right decision. Although Tate being forced to quit was bad, the outcome was worth it. *And now she's fulfilled,* Liza thought. *And I have the Tate that I always wanted.*

ADMIRING the blue streamers and gold-colored balloons she and Marty put all around the gym's foyer, Tate felt a satisfaction her old job never brought. *Because it's my gym,* she thought. *Something I can control, and all my hard work will be for the betterment of the business Nikki and I now own.* She looked at the blonde woman in the wheelchair talking to Vivian at the mocktail table. Although one arm and one leg remained in a cast, it was good to see her friend out of her apartment. Because they had been meeting every day to go over plans for the gym, Tate saw some of the things her friend couldn't hide. The last few weeks had been harder on Nikki than she let on, but Tate knew Nikki still suffered from a lot of pain caused by her injuries. Only the use of pain medication seemed to give her relief and keep her functional.

As Tate was about to check that everything in the weight room was ready for her demonstration later, her cell phone rang on the counter beside her. Looking, she saw it was from a number she recognized but never expected to see again— her old boss, Chad. Curious more than anything, she answered. "Hello."

"Tate, how are you?" the man asked, making Tate lift her eyebrows. *Why is he asking me that?* she wondered. *Or even calling at all?*

"Never better," she answered. "What is this about?"

Chad cleared his throat. "I'm glad you picked up," he said. "Some things have come to light at the firm, and I wanted to tell you that the role of Vice President of Mergers and Acquisitions has opened up. I'd like to offer it to you."

Shocked, Tate didn't know quite how to answer. A part of her had longed for exactly that type of call. Even though she loved buying the gym and working to make it better than ever, it was still scary. When she worked at the firm, she had a steady and reliable income, something that wasn't going to be the case with a small business. Yet now that it was happening, all she wanted to do was laugh at Chad's offer.

Tate smiled widely. "Not on your life," she answered. "I've decided to go a different direction with my career. One where I am appreciated and makes me feel validated."

"Tate, you were always—" Chad started, but Tate had heard enough.

"Don't bother, Chad," she said. "I've made up my mind. I heard from HR, and I know my claims were validated. Just count your blessings that I haven't decided to sue the firm, or maybe even you and Aurora."

"Now, wait a minute—" Chad started again.

With a shake of her head, Tate realized she truly was done with that chapter of her life. "I need to go, but good luck with the firm." She hung up without waiting for a response because she had better things to do.

The door to the gym opened, and a beaming Liza walked in with Allie and Rey. "The new sign looks so good out there," she said, glancing around the room. "And so does all of this." She crossed to Tate and kissed her. "You've done so much, and worked so hard, and it shows. I couldn't be prouder of you."

Taking Liza's hand, Tate looked at her friends who had gathered around her as Vivian handed out mocktails. The doors to the gym for the grand reopening would happen in a few minutes, but she needed a second to absorb it all. Her fiancée, Liza. Her gym with her best friend, Nikki. Plus, Allie and Vivian, Marty and Rey. People she cared about most in the world. "Thank you to each of you," she said looking from one to the other. "This never would have happened without you." She held up her glass. "So, I propose a toast." Everyone lifted their glass. "To the power of our friendship. May we always be together. Cheers!"

"Cheers," the others said, touching glasses, and as Tate drank the fabulous mocktail, the future never looked brighter.

THE END
Want more?
Sign up for my newsletter
(https://landing.mailerlite.com/webforms/landing/r2b5s6)
to keep tabs on what I am writing next.

## ABOUT THE AUTHOR

Bestselling author KC Luck writes action adventure, contemporary romance, and lesbian fiction. Writing is her passion, and nothing energizes her more than creating new characters facing trials and tribulations in a complex plot. Whether it is apocalypse, horror, or a little naughty, with every story, KC tries to add her own unique twist. She has written over a dozen books (which include *The Darkness Series* and *Everybody Needs a Hero*) and multiple short stories across many genres. KC is active in the LGBTQ+ community and is the founder of the collective iReadIndies.

To receive updates on KC Luck's books, please consider subscribing to her mailing list (https://landing.mailerlite.com/webforms/landing/r2b5s6). Also, KC Luck is always thrilled to hear from her readers (kc.luck.author@gmail.com)

To follow KC Luck, you can find her at: www.kc-luck.com

## THANK YOU

Enjoy this book?
You can make a big difference.

Honest reviews of my books help bring them to the attention of other readers. If you've enjoyed this story, I would be incredibly grateful if you could spend a couple minutes leaving a review (it can be as short as you like) on the book's Amazon and Goodreads pages.

## ALSO BY KC LUCK

Rescue Her Heart

Save Her Heart

Welcome to Ruby's

Back to Ruby's

Darkness Falls

Darkness Remains

Darkness United

Wind Dancer

Darkness San Francisco

The Lesbian Billionaires Club

The Lesbian Billionaires Seduction

The Lesbian Billionaires Last Hope

Venandi

What the Heart Sees

Everybody Needs a Hero

Can't Fight Love

Where Love Leads

One Last Sunset

IREADINDIES

This author is part of iReadIndies, a collective of self-published independent authors of sapphic literature. Please visit our website at iReadIndies.com for more information and to find links to the books published by our authors.

Printed in Great Britain
by Amazon